INTERVIEW

with

JOAB

MICHAEL
BRASWELL

WIPF & STOCK · Eugene, Oregon

Resource Publications
A division of Wipf and Stock Publishers
199 W 8th Ave, Suite 3
Eugene, OR 97401

Interview with Joab
By Braswell, Michael
Copyright © 2014 by Braswell, Michael All rights reserved.
Softcover ISBN-13: 978-1-6667-3464-5
Hardcover ISBN-13: 978-1-6667-9072-6
eBook ISBN-13: 978-1-6667-9073-3
Publication date 8/31/2021
Previously published by Ellechor Media & Associates LLC, 2014

Table of Contents

ACKNOWLEDGMENTS

In addition to again thanking Tony Campolo, Jack Higgs, Michael Helms and Mark Jones for reviewing and writing endorsements for the manuscript, I also want to express appreciation to Steve Bader for reading and commenting on an early version as well. I appreciate the encouragement from the publisher Rochelle Carter and copy editor, Veronika Walker. Most importantly, I am grateful for the continuing love and support of my wife, Susan.

INTRODUCTION

INTERVIEW WITH JOAB provides a "what if" perspective as a way of expanding Bible stories and their themes into lessons and points of reflection for contemporary Christians. Why did the villains and heroes act as they did? What motivated them? How could their outcomes have been different? What can we learn from their experiences that have relevance for our lives?

Why did Joseph's brothers want to kill him? Why was Caiaphas so threatened by Jesus' ministry of healing and "good news" for the poor and downtrodden? What about Judas—what reasons besides the thirty pieces of silver may he have had for betraying Jesus? What about characters like Jacob who, in a manner of speaking, was both a hero and a villain? What led him to deceive his father and betray his brother? Then there was Joab, David's loyal army commander who also killed Absalom, David's son— what led him down the path of ruin?

What about people like the prodigal son and Gomer, Hosea's wife, and the adulteress who would have been stoned had it not been for Jesus' intervention—how might they have responded to their second chances?

Of course, no one knows for sure what the final outcome was for any of these characters. We can imagine both tragic and sorrowful consequences for those who chose poorly, and the gratitude of those persons who embraced the mercy that was offered them.

Following each story is the Scriptural reference which inspired the story and brief comments which examine and explore themes and issues of the story that relate to the challenges of contemporary living. The commentaries are followed by a series of questions that encourage personal reflection and group discussion about the stories and how each offers lessons and insights for us today.

1

THE BLESSING

THE ANTELOPE STOOD silent and alert, frozen in place next to the small stream. The vapor that exhaled from its flared nostrils in the early morning chill was the only evidence of the antelope's presence.

A twig snapped and the frightened animal leaped across the stream toward safety, catching only a fleeting glimpse of the bronze-tipped arrow hurtling through the fog toward its intended target.

———

"That was some shot. And in the fog, at that—right through the heart," Naham said to his hunting partner as he rotated the haunch of fresh antelope over the cook-fire. "The others will be jealous when they return from the hunt. One shot, one antelope."

Esau smiled to himself. He and Naham had been friends—the best of friends—for many years. As usual, his friend exaggerated, but the truth was Esau had always been an excellent hunter and tracker. From the time he had been a young boy, he had always felt more comfortable in the forest and the wilds than in the village. On the backside of middle age, Esau led by example. A man of few words, his actions were legend. As a young man, he had killed a bear with a stone axe. Several years later, six Canaanite bandits who tried to steal his goat herd had met a sudden and brutal end by his hand.

Esau accepted the piece of venison Naham cut from the slow-roasted haunch. Naham had become like a brother to him, and the fact that Naham had a head for numbers and managed Esau's property suited Esau just fine.

"How's the venison, oh great hunter?"

Esau looked at his friend squatting next to the fire and smiled. "Not bad. Better than the last time."

Naham threw a stick at Esau in jest, and both men laughed.

Esau pondered the morning mist. "My father always loved venison."

Naham stood up from the cook-fire. "That he did, especially that stew you used to cook." He paused. "I still can't figure out how Jacob was able to trick him with the goat stew, not to mention the hides he covered his arms with."

Introduction

Esau turned to Naham, a somber look returning to his face. "My father, Isaac, was old and blind...near the end of his life."

Naham picked up a jar of water and drank from it. "That was some number your brother did on you. He was always a slick one, a real wheeler-dealer."

Esau threw the remnants of his venison to two of his hunting dogs, who yelped with delight at their good fortune. "I was always my father's favorite. My mother loved Jacob best. There was never a better man than my father. He got along with everyone. Never held a grudge. He could negotiate his way out of just about anything."

Esau accepted the jar of water from the out-stretched hands of Naham and took a long drink. "I don't have my father's temperament. I understand the forest, but with people, I see things in black and white. Good or bad, I return as given."

"No kidding," Naham replied. "Like the time those Canaanites tried to steal your goat herd. It's a wonder you didn't skin Jacob alive."

Esau looked out at nothing in particular. "I probably would have if I had caught him. It was my brother's good fortune that my mother sent him to our Uncle Laban."

Naham added some more kindling to the cook-fire. "I guess being a 'mama's boy' does have its advantages."

Esau squinted at Naham and took another long pull from the water jar.

"In some ways, yes—in other ways, no. Father let me grow into a man, let me hunt, roam the forest, and spend time with my friends. I didn't always please him, like the time I took Adah and Aholibamah for my wives. I knew he was upset and didn't approve, but I was headstrong. Still, Father didn't admonish me. He made sure there was peace between me and him.

"Jacob wasn't so lucky with my mother. She hovered over him like a crow from the day he was born. Kept him out of the forest whenever she could. He liked to go hunting with me, but she...." Esau exhaled and stopped. "Doesn't really matter. Although I was born first, my brother was born right behind me. His hand grabbed my heel. Guess he finally tripped me—got me out of the way. Never would have believed he would hold me to that oath. A birthright for a bowl of porridge!"

Esau shook his head. Naham was silent.

"Yes, ol' Jacob did the deed. He tricked me out of my birthright and stole my blessing, but my mother put him up to it. It broke my father's heart. Wouldn't be surprised if it didn't hasten his death." Esau stared at the campfire. "Wish I could see him again."

Naham could see a cloud of sorrow descend upon Esau, that he still grieved over the past. "As they say, 'what's done is done.' And if I do say so, you, my good friend Esau, have done quite well. The flocks of sheep and goats, the forests and plentiful wild game, and the fresh springs, not to mention that your clan has become strong and prosperous....Travelers have intimated on more than one occasion that Jacob, with all his tricks and maneuvering, hasn't had such an easy road."

Esau turned to his friend with the cracked hint of a smile. "True enough. It seems as though my brother, the trickster, found his uncle Laban a more talented trickster than he was."

Naham chuckled. "It took him 14 years of Laban's shenanigans for Jacob to win his daughter Rachel's hand in marriage."

Both men turned to the sound of the rest of their hunting party returning to camp. Naham grinned at Esau. "I wonder how many arrows they had to use."

———

The campfires of 400 men flickered in the cool of a summer's evening. Scattered groups laughed, sang, and jostled about after the evening meal. Esau and Naham stood on a ridge overlooking the Jabbok River, observing the sight of a campfire less than a mile away.

"So it comes full circle," Naham said. "Will Jacob reap the harvest of deceit he sowed those many years ago when he stole your birthright and blessing? You've killed men for less."

"True enough," Esau replied, pointing to the campfires on the other side of the river located a good distance from his brother's lone campsite. "He is afraid, so he sends his wives and children back across the river so they can flee should we attack."

Naham took a small loaf of barley bread from a pouch slung over his shoulder and tore off a piece. "The tribute he sent you was substantial, if not excessive. Fine herds of cattle and goats, linen...."

Esau began to chew on the bread Naham offered him. "Such generosity is another sign of fear."

Naham popped a piece of bread in his mouth. "First light will come soon."

Esau looked to the east. "Yes, it won't be long. In the morning, my brother and I will meet."

"Will you go out alone to meet him?"

Esau smiled to himself. "No, I will take you and 100 of my strongest warriors with me."

Naham stopped chewing for a moment and looked at Esau. "So, justice it will be. Jacob and his servants won't last long against us."

Esau continued, smiling. "Not justice. Just a little overdue satisfaction, watching my brother squirm as you and I and 100 warriors pay him a visit."

Introduction

Naham began to smile as well. "I see. I see. I'm not so sure I would be as generous and forgiving had my brother stolen my birthright. And my blessing. And spread the word that God had ordained that my people would serve him and his children's children."

Esau's smile disappeared. "I can't foretell the future. Don't know who will end up serving who. What I do know is that God's been good to me. My brother stole my property and blessing but not my father's heart. More like he broke it. I received my father's blessing in the look of his eye every time he saw me coming. Nobody can steal that. Besides, even though Jacob did what he did, he's still my brother. What good is a grudge as old as mine? What purpose can it serve except to dishonor my good father's memory?"

Esau and Naham grew silent before the reddish-rose streaks of dawn. They watched a solitary figure emerge from his tent next to the river and stoke his campfire.

"I dreamed of my father last night," Esau said.

Naham looked at his friend. "Did he say anything?"

"He looked at me for a long time and then he smiled."

"But did he say anything?"

"He said, 'You cook good venison.'"

COMMENTS

Genesis 25:21-34; Genesis 26:34; Genesis 27; Genesis 28:6-9; Genesis 33.

The story of how Jacob with the help of his mother, Rebekah, stole his brother's birthright and his father's blessing has been told and retold for generations. Manipulation, deceit, and betrayal are as much a problem in today's world as it was in Jacob and Esau's. The times may have changed, but the stories often remain the same.

Receiving a blessing is an ancient rite that has strong reverberations in modern life. How many times do we hear or read about a violent criminal who grew up without a father? There are many reasons, of course, a person turns to violence. Children raised by their mother and sometimes even grandparents often grow into very well-adjusted adults; still, as in Jacob's time, a father's blessing is very important. Although it may not seem like it at times, sons and daughters seek their parents' approval and attention in one way or another. For sons and fathers, such approval takes on a special significance. This was particularly true concerning Isaac's blessing, since it included resources such as grain, wine, and land. Tradition held that the eldest son received his father's blessing. Becoming head of the household also meant all others in Isaac's family were to be subservient to that son's leadership.

What followed in Esau's case was enough deceit and betrayal to make Shakespeare proud. Jacob was his mothers favorite, Esau his father's. Rachel's cunning trumped family tradition. Though Jacob received the blessing and all its wealth through ill-gotten means, the prize came at a heavy price. He lost his father's respect and had to flee for his life from his brother's wrath, never to see his mother again.

In today's families, favoritism can still tear the fabric of family life apart. Brother against brother, sister against sister—all seeking their parents' approval even at the cost of fellowship, affection, and intimacy. It is always sad to see elderly people who still carry the scars of such dysfunction, when a few words of love and encouragement from parents long passed could have changed the course of their children's lives. What this story offers us, if it offers us anything, is a reminder of the potential consequences of favoritism and the importance of making sure all of our children

Introduction

receive an honest blessing from us—one that includes our concerns, but more importantly, our love and encouragement for each of them.

QUESTIONS

1. Research suggests that twins are often very close in a unique and intimate way. That closeness obviously wasn't the case with Esau and Jacob. What do you think went wrong? What could Rachel and Isaac, their parents, have done differently that could have avoided many of their family problems?

2. Can you think of examples in your experience and observation where favoritism has caused pain and suffering in a family situation?

3. In spite of our faults and mistakes as parents and siblings, family hurts do often heal over time. Apologies are made and accepted. What role did God play in blessing both Esau and Jacob and repairing their broken relationship?

4. Can you recall times when God's hand was apparent in healing and restoring broken family relationships in your life?

NOTES:

_____

_____

_____

_____

_____

_____

_____

_____

_____

Introduction

2

LITTLE BROTHER

Someone's coming!" Simeon shouted from his perch on a rock out-crop-ping some thirty feet off the ground. Of all Jacob's sons, Simeon could see best in the distance. Although his eyesight was nothing short of un-canny, his brothers liked to pick at him.

"You sure it's not another one of your mirages?" Levi shouted back as he leaned on his staff, watching the large flock of sheep graze below him. Judah, who was spreading the animal skin on the ground where he and his brothers would eat their noonday meal, laughed at Levi's retort. Levi watched Judah gather wood for the cook-fire. "What's on the menu for to-day's feast, brother Judah?"

Judah smiled. "Your choice—lamb stew, or if that doesn't suit your taste, stewed lamb."

Levi chuckled. "It's still a long time until the sun reaches high noon. I'll think about it and get back to you."

Reuben, the eldest, and his half-brother, Asher, arrived from the south-ern pasture.

Judah stood and offered his brothers a skin filled with fresh water. "How goes it?"

Reuben drank deeply and handed the skin to Asher. "The herd looks to be in pretty good shape. Two or three are missing. Saw some signs of a jackal nearby—maybe more than one. Asher and I will need to scout out some new grazing areas later this morning. I think there may be some de-cent pasture just over the ridge to the west of us."

Judah nodded and looked in the direction where Simeon had pointed out two men approaching. He could barely see the two distant forms moving in their direction. "Simeon spotted a couple of visitors coming our way."

Reuben plugged the water-skin. "Friend or foe?"

"Simeon! Can you make out anything about the travelers?" Judah called out to his brother.

Simeon cradled his hands over his eyes to block out the sun, straining to get a better look. He looked down at his brothers, suddenly troubled and crestfallen. "I'm afraid so."

"Do we need to arm ourselves?" Reuben asked.

"That depends," Simeon replied.

"On what?"

"On whether you want to use them on a snitch who happens to be your brother and the favorite, spoiled brat son of your father."

Levi joined his other brothers as Simeon scrambled down from his lookout. "Issachar and Zebulun and I will be in from the western pasture for the noonday meal about the time Joseph and the other fellow will be arriving," Levi said. "Once we send the stranger on his way, we can take care of the 'dreamer' and his coat of many colors once and for all. We've been talking about a chance like this for a long time. If we don't seize this opportunity, we may never get another."

Simeon wiped the sweat from his brow. "Levi's right. This is our chance —what we've been waiting for. The 'little prince' has already ratted us out more than once to the old man."

Judah stroked his beard. "I don't know. Joseph has gotten us in trouble with Father, and there is no question he thinks he's better than us. But killing him? He's still our blood."

"That may be so," Levi interjected, "but with the way things are going, it wouldn't surprise me if our so-called father doesn't end up defying tradition and leaving everything to the little brat."

Simeon's eyes narrowed as he studied his brothers. "I'll do it. I'll do the deed."

Levi turned to Reuben. "Why haven't you spoken, Reuben? No one suffered more at the hand of our father than you when Joseph told him about us meeting up with those Canaanite women against his wishes."

"It would kill him," Reuben replied in a quiet, steady voice. "If we kill Joseph, it would break our father's heart. He would never get over it. Besides, it's no secret that I slept with his concubine, Bilhah, after a night of too much wine. That, more than any other disobedience, has chilled the heart of my father toward me. Still, we need to remember: whatever harm we do to Joseph, we do twice over to our father."

Levi placed his hand on Reuben's shoulder. "Maybe, maybe not. If the 'little prince' wasn't around, Father may realize that he has other sons he can depend on."

Simeon pointed to two nearby cisterns. "After we kill him, we can throw his body in one of those cisterns."

"We can smear goat's blood on his coat and tell the old man that a wild animal killed and ate him. How's that for a dream?" Levi added.

"Sounds like a plan," Simeon grinned.

"We know what Zebulun and Issachar think," Levi continued. "They wanted to ambush Joseph a couple of weeks ago when he was walking by the stream northwest of the main camp. What's your take, Asher?"

Asher shrugged. "I can see both sides. I don't like Joseph getting the best of everything and not having to work like the rest of us, but Reuben's right. Father would never get over it."

"Asher, can't you ever think for yourself? Can't you ever have an opinion of your own without imitating your big brother, Reuben? You will always be the runt of the litter until you stand on your own two feet," Simeon sneered.

Reuben's stern look brought Simeon's taunt to a standstill. "We've still got an hour or two before Joseph arrives and Zebulun and Issachar return from their fields. We need to wait on them before deciding," Reuben said.

"We already know—"

Reuben interrupted Simeon. "Doesn't matter. Whatever we end up doing will be on all our heads, so we all need to decide together. Besides, that will give Asher and me time to scout out the new pasture. We're losing daylight and we could risk the entire flock if we don't find safe pasture by nightfall." Reuben looked at each of his brothers solemnly. "Are we all in agreement that nothing will happen to Joseph until we are all present?"

Judah nodded his head in agreement. Levi and Simeon reluctantly followed with their assent.

"Do I have your oath?" Reuben added, looking at Judah.

Judah and the others nodded once more.

Reuben and Asher left to look for new grazing ground.

"Simeon, get back to your lookout. Levi, make yourself useful and get me some leeks, lentils, and garlic for the stew while I finish dressing the lamb," Judah instructed his other two brothers.

"Reuben's a wimp when it comes to Father!" Simeon shouted back as he climbed back up to his lookout.

Levi dropped the ingredients Judah had requested into the pot that was beginning to simmer. "We can't let Reuben and Asher ruin our chance just because Reuben's afraid of the old man. There are five of us to two of them. If our other brothers were here, they would even be more outnumbered."

Judah looked up at Levi from where he was cutting pieces of lamb. "Reuben's acting like who he is—the eldest son." He looked at Levi and smiled. "Calm down. Everything will work out."

Reuben and Asher walked in silence until Asher spoke.

"It doesn't look good."

Reuben said nothing and continued to chew on a piece of grass.

"What are we going to do, Reuben?"

Little Brother

Reuben spit the stalk of grass from his mouth. "Buy time for now. There will be some kind of showdown. They all despise Joseph—especially Simeon and Levi, who are closest in age to him and the most jealous. They will be the hotheads, the ones most likely to move against him first. Zebulun and Issachar hate Joseph almost as much, but they are followers."

"What about Judah?" Asher queried.

"It's hard to read Judah. He probably wouldn't mind getting rid of Joseph. Still, he's the smartest of that bunch, and he's not so filled with hate."

"And what about Joseph?" Asher continued, rubbing sweat from his brow.

"Joseph could be the wild card," Reuben replied. "I've tried to talk to him on several occasions, but I don't think I got through. He's oblivious most of the time to how his actions affect the others."

"He thinks he's better than us," Asher interjected.

Reuben paused before responding. "In a way that's true. That's what he's been taught by Father and his servants. But he's not really mean-spirited. More naive than selfish. He's still our little brother. The key thing for you and me is to check out the new pasture and get back to camp before Joseph arrives."

"So things don't get out of hand," Asher replied.

"That's right, brother. So things don't get out of hand."

The stranger that brought the wandering Joseph to his brothers disappeared over the ridge, stocked with provisions and a full wineskin—his reward for delivering Joseph.

"The stew smells good. When do we eat?" Joseph asked as he bent over the simmering pot, taking in its pungent aroma.

Judah threw a handful of dill into the pot and wiped his hands on his tunic. "Not just yet, Joseph. Why have you come?"

"Checking on us again?" Simeon queried sarcastically.

Joseph looked directly at Simeon. "As a matter of fact, I have come to check on you and report back to Father."

Issachar glared at his younger brother. "Check on us, or rat us out like you did last time?"

"I told Father the truth. No more, no less. I did what he asked of me. Your own actions got you into trouble, not mine," Joseph replied as he picked up a skin filled with water and drank from it.

A dark cloud descended on the group of brothers surrounding Joseph. Although no one spoke, the looks on their faces reflected a menace that even Joseph couldn't ignore.

"Where are Reuben and Asher?"

Judah returned to the stew pot and stirred its ingredients with a wooden spoon. "They're checking out some new pasture."

Levi looked at Joseph with a coldness that made him uneasy. "Not sure when they will be back. How 'bout you, little brother? What are you sure of? Still think all of us are going to bow down to you? Be your servants? Still dreaming those princely dreams?"

Joseph looked at Zebulun and Issachar, who stood next to Levi with their arms crossed. He could feel the hair stand up on the back of his neck like the time two years ago when he was stalked by a wolf. "They were dreams. Sometimes I dream. You all know that. I told you and Father what I dreamed—what I saw. I can't help what it was. I saw what I saw. Who knows if it will come true? It was a dream."

Levi knocked the water skin out of Joseph's hand. "What you're getting ready to have is a bad dream—a nightmare that you won't wake up from."

"That's right!" Simeon slapped Joseph with his open hand, knocking him to the ground.

The others converged on him, kicking and pummeling Joseph, giving vent to their pent- up anger and frustration.

"Let's kill him!" Simeon shouted as the beating intensified. "Let's do it!"

Suddenly, the top end of a shepherd's staff cracked against Simeon's back and sent him sprawling in the dust with a yelp. Judah grabbed Joseph by his tunic and jerked him to his feet.

Joseph stood behind Judah, blood dripping from his mouth and a cut over his eye, trying to catch his breath. "Father will be very angry with you!" Joseph shouted in a hoarse voice.

"Shut up," Judah hissed.

An exasperated Levi gestured wildly at Judah. "Are you crazy? This is our best chance to rid ourselves of him. You know he's going to tell the old man what we've done to him. We don't have a choice. It's him or us."

Judah planted his staff squarely in front of him as he eyed his angry brothers. "I don't care for him anymore than the rest of you do. But we promised Reuben we wouldn't kill him—we wouldn't shed his blood—we wouldn't decide what to do until we were all together." Judah pointed at Zebulun and Issachar. "You two strip him down to his loincloth and put him in that dry cistern next to where our supplies are covered. Levi...you and Simeon get that wheat flour and cook some bread for the stew."

Little Brother

"The new grazing spot was farther than I imagined it to be," Reuben commented as he observed the sun's position. "Joseph should have arrived by now."

"That's not a good thing," Asher replied.

"No. We've got to push harder. There's no telling what they've done to Joseph."

"Stew's about ready!" Simeon called out to his brothers.

While the others begin to eat their noon meal, Levi scooped up a mouthful of stew and walked over to the cistern Joseph had been thrown into. He peered down at Joseph. "That's some good stew, little brother. How's the dreaming down there? See anybody bowing down to you in the bottom of that cistern? How does it feel to be without your fancy coat?"

"That's enough, Levi. Get up on Simeon's lookout and see if you can spot Reuben and Asher. We need to keep an eye out for them."

"Who made you the boss, Judah? You're not the eldest," a sullen Levi retorted.

"Do you want to talk to my staff the way Simeon did?" Judah replied firmly.

Judah walked over to the cistern and looked down at Joseph.

"How are you doing?"

"Not so good," Joseph responded. "Are you going to let them kill me?"

"Maybe, maybe not," Judah replied as he passed a bowl of stew and chunk of bread down to his brother. "Depends."

"Depends on what?" Joseph asked as he hungrily spooned the stew into his mouth with the bread.

"I'm not sure at this point," Judah replied. "I don't want your blood on my head, but you can't go home. Too much has happened. You'd tell Father."

Joseph said nothing. He knew Judah was right—he would tell Father.

Judah passed a jar of water down to Joseph. "Truth is, except for Reuben and Asher, your brothers hate you and want to see you dead."

"What about you, Judah?" Joseph asked.

Judah paused before answering. "Don't know for sure. Can't say as I like you much. You get the best of everything and whether you mean to or not, you lord it over us, make us feel small and angry—second best. Don't really want to see you killed, but don't know how long I can keep the rest of them settled down. Reuben and Asher need to hurry back before things get more out of hand than they already are."

Judah chewed on a piece of bread as he watched his brothers devour the stew he had prepared. "Be sure to leave some for Reuben and Asher," he reminded them.

"Judah!" Levi shouted. "Looks like a caravan of Ishmaelites coming from Gilead. About half an hour out. Their camels are loaded."

Zebulun spoke through a mouthful of stew. "Probably headed to Egypt."

Judah looked at the horizon. No sign of Reuben and Asher. And he could hear Simeon doing his best with animated whispers to get Zebulun and Issachar to join him and Levi in their murderous desires. From the sounds of the conversations, one didn't have to be a psychic to see that he was enjoying some measure of success, although it was hard to tell just how much.

Judah stroked his beard. There were few choices. None of them good. Without the presence of Reuben and Asher, it would be difficult for him to stand against his four other brothers much longer. And as irritating and arrogant as Joseph could be, Judah didn't want his little brother's blood on his hands, not to mention the affect Joseph's death would have on his father. Judah was quieter, less talkative than his older brother, Reuben. But when it was time to act, he didn't often second guess himself. He carefully considered all the options available to him, and was then inclined to act decisively.

"Brothers, gather 'round. I have a solution to our problem."

Levi scrambled down from his perch, and the others left the remnants of their meal on the leather ground-cloth and huddled around Judah.

"The Ishamaelites are traders, are they not?"

"They are that," Issachar replied, the other brothers grunting their agreement.

Judah continued. "They don't just trade in spices and myrrh. They are also known to trade on occasion for slaves."

"You want to sell Joseph to the Ishmaelites?" Zebulun queried.

Judah crossed his arms. "That's right. We get rid of our problem. Like Levi suggested, we smear Joseph's coat with goat's blood and tell our father he was killed by a wild animal. We don't carry our brother's blood on our heads. And we even make a little profit we can divide among ourselves."

"I'd rather kill him," Levi calmly replied.

"Me too," chimed in Simeon.

The four brothers grew quiet as they contemplated Judah's plan.

Finally, Zebulun and Issachar spoke in favor of Judah's plan. Levi and Simeon had little choice but to go along...although they still got to experience the pleasure of watching their younger brother stumble into the hot desert afternoon, tethered with a rope to a feisty camel loaded with supplies.

Judah divided the twenty shekels of silver the Ishmaelite traders had paid for Joseph into equal shares for his brothers.

Little Brother

When Reuben and Asher found, upon returning to camp, that Joseph had been sold into slavery, Reuben collapsed, beating his chest and tearing his clothes in grief. He couldn't be consoled by the others, even Judah. Later that night, a forlorn Reuben sat by the fire, staring blankly into the flames. The other brothers except for Judah, were either asleep or keeping watch over the herds.

Judah threw another stick of wood into the fire, sat down next to Reuben, and said nothing. Finally, he turned to his brother.

"Would you rather Joseph be dead?"

Reuben continued staring into the fire. "He was our little brother—our responsibility."

"You're right, but at least he's alive. He didn't die at the hand of Simeon or Levi."

Reuben turned and looked at Judah with a combination of bitterness and sorrow. "Who knows whether Joseph is alive or dead? Either way, he will be dead to our father because of our lies and deeds."

"It seemed the best of a bad set of choices," Judah replied.

Reuben returned his gaze to the fire. "It is foolish to think that things will be better with Joseph gone. If you think life was difficult with Joseph and his fancy coat around, wait and see how difficult life will be with him gone—with our father's spirit broken." Reuben put his head in hands. "Things will never be the same. Our future is less certain than ever. Who knows where it will take us?"

COMMENTS

Genesis 30:24; 37:3-36

Joseph was the youngest of Jacob's sons, and enjoyed all the attention and privileges that a youngest child often receives. Joseph was also very bright. As intelligent as he was, he was apparently equally lacking in tactfulness—especially with his brothers.

Sometimes when a child is favored by one or both parents at the expense of his or her other siblings, resentment—or worse—can be the result. Where such feelings exist, psychological and even physical violence in one form or another can follow.

Sibling rivalry is nothing new, and has been an issue for families to deal with since Cain and Abel. What starts in childhood is often carried forward into adulthood. Virginia Satir, a family therapist, once wrote that, "Adults are children grown big."

As parents, there are things we can do to mitigate the rivalry that exists between our *sons* and daughters. We can find a niche where each child can be affirmed in his or her own unique way, and reward them for cooperation and kindness rather than just competing with others for this or that prize. Competing with oneself—doing the very best one can do—is important, but when we are driven to the extreme in competing with others, especially our siblings, false pride and disappointment are often the inevitable consequences.

Joseph was the youngest and most favored among his brothers. While bright and gifted, he also wore his "coat of many colors" with pride. Birth order research suggests that the youngest child often has the closest emotional bond to his or her parents. The oldest child typically often feels the most responsible and is often the most achievement-oriented. We can see those characteristics in Joseph and Reuben.

In today's world, many of us are a part of a "blended" family. Practically speaking, given that Jacob had several wives and concubines, the same was true of Jacob's family. We are told that Joseph was the son of Rachel, Jacob's favorite wife, which only made matters worse as far as his brothers were concerned. Joseph's "special coat" was like waving a red flag to constantly remind his brothers who was number one in their father's eyes. All sons yearn for their father's affirmation as well as their mother's. When they are denied such reassurance, self-loathing and anger turned outward toward others can be the tragic result. As stated previously, sons are often uniquely sensitive to their father's opinion. It is important that fathers and mothers identify each of their children's special gifts and talents and encourage them to reach their full potential.

QUESTIONS

1. It is often said that the sins of the father are often passed down to his sons. This can also be true regarding the sins of the mother. Jacob was his mother's favorite. Joseph was Jacob's favorite. What lessons may Jacob not have learned from his own unfortunate experiences with his mother that impacted his sons?

2. In hindsight, how could Jacob possibly have defused the rivalry between his sons? Could his treatment of Joseph in relation to his other sons be an example of the "sins of his mother" regarding his brother, Esau finding expression in his own life?

3. Can you think of other examples in the Bible of intense sibling rivalry between brothers?

4. Anger and jealousy can often result in spontaneous acts of violence and destruction that have devastating, lifelong consequences. Can you think of any modern news-worthy examples?

5. Even Jesus' disciples at the Last Supper were concerned about who was His favorite. How do you think Jesus would resolve the issue of rivalry? Since we are all God's children, why does rivalry have no place in God's kingdom?

NOTES:

_____

_____

_____

_____

_____

_____

_____

Little Brother

_____

_____

_____

_____

_____

_____

_____

_____

_____

3

SECOND CHANCE LOVE

IT WAS A hot, dusty afternoon. The smell of cheap wine and even cheaper perfume engulfed Hosea as he entered the brothel. Sounds of laughter and practiced moans of delight echoed from the small rooms to his left and his right. A dog barked in the street as Hosea wiped the perspiration from his forehead with the back of his hand. He could feel the beginning of another headache, and a knot forming in the pit of his stomach.

Hosea had tried to do Jehovah's bidding as he was instructed. It had seemed an impossible task, but he was no quitter. But now, tired and torn with worry, he felt like giving up.

A squat, sweaty mound of a man swaggered up to Hosea and turned his lips up into the timeless smile of the pimp. His practiced grin didn't quite fit the calculating gaze of his dark, narrow eyes. He extended his hand as if greeting an old friend. Hosea ignored the man's gesture and instead thrust a bag of money into his outstretched hand. The proprietor of the brothel shrugged indifferently and poured the contents onto the top of a small wooden table, carefully counting each shekel. Without looking up from the money, he pointed to a small room at the end of the hall.

Gomer would be waiting there.

Hosea paused at the entrance and looked at her through strands of beads hanging from the doorway.

Gomer sat on a pallet, staring at the wall across from her. She had put on some weight, and there was a small scar on the left side of her forehead, the result of only God knew what. Still, in spite of the heavy rouge and painted eyes and everything else that had happened between them, Hosea felt the breath catch in his throat and the palms of his hands grow moist.

He pushed aside the beads and walked into the room.

"How are you?"

Gomer looked at the man standing before her.

"How do you think I am?"

Hosea sat down next to her. "Not so good."

Gomer said nothing as she stared at a crack in the wall.

The silence was thick and heavy between them.

Hosea cleared his throat. "I've come for you. I paid Obeth for your freedom."

"That so?" Gomer replied, continuing to stare at the wall. "Maybe you should try to get a refund. I'm not worth what I used to be."

Hosea ignored her remarks as he swatted at a fly buzzing between them. "You can come home now. It's the right thing to do…to get you out of here. You're still the mother of my children."

"You don't say?" Gomer replied laconically. "Sounds like another mission from God to me. Good old Hosea—always trying to do the right thing." She swatted at the stubborn fly buzzing around her face and said as much to herself as to Hosea, "You never loved me anyway."

Hosea winced. "How can you say that, Gomer? I married you. We had three children."

Gomer watched the fly crawl along the crack in the wall. "God told you to."

Hosea leaned forward. "So what if He did? I gave you a life, a family—a home."

"You gave me what?" Gomer turned to face Hosea, her dark eyes blazing. "I was a whore who bore you three children. You paraded us around as examples of Israel's unfaithfulness to God and His judgment upon our people. How do you think that felt—being on display day in and day out? Having to listen to the self-righteous whispers of the village wives and mothers? I heard and saw what they thought of me. And your poor sons and daughter!"

Gomer continued, her voice rising. "What about your children? Giving them names that mean 'punishment,' 'no mercy,' and 'not mine'! Did you not hear the ridicule they endured from the other children?"

Hosea looked at his hands and sighed deeply. "I know it has been hard on you…and the children. I was trying to do what God called me to do—to be faithful and obedient to—"

"Yes, yes," Gomer interrupted. "Faithful and obedient, doing the right thing, orders from on high. I've heard it all before."

"But I have paid for your freedom. I gave Obeth everything I had for your freedom!" Hosea responded, gesturing in earnest. "What else can I do?"

Gomer looked at Hosea quietly before responding. "Nothing, I guess. Your heart belongs to God. He called and you answered. He instructed and you acted. But though you can buy me—as you have found out before—does not mean that you can keep me. Buying and keeping are different things."

The silence returned. Gomer returned her gaze to the crack in the wall, and Hosea hunched forward, looking at his outstretched hands resting on his knees.

He finally spoke. His voice was tired. "I know it hasn't been easy. Maybe it never will be. His will can be hard. And my heart does belong to Him." Hosea closed his eyes and paused for a moment, choosing his words carefully. "My heart also belongs to you."

With a subtle turn of her head, Gomer's eyes shifted toward the sound of Hosea's voice.

Hosea bowed his head and whispered, "Gomer, I love you. Will you give me another chance?"

Gomer slowly turned to face her husband.

Hosea leaned toward her. "I know people talk about you. They talk about me, too. They think I'm crazy for marrying you—for loving you. They will never understand that the heart has reasons of its own. With you, His will and my desire have always been the same. He sent me to the brothel to find a wife, but I chose you." Hosea looked deep into Gomer's eyes. "My heart still chooses you. I want you to come home."

Gomer's eyes glistened. She slowly reached out and wrapped her fingers around the palm of his outstretched hand.

COMMENTS

Hosea 1-3

Have you ever known someone who in their fervor to do good, secure their family's future, or, in Hosea's case, serve the Lord, ended up causing harm and distress to the very people who meant the most to them? Like the old saying goes, "It is the cobbler's children who often have no shoes."

The story of Hosea and Gomer is not just a story about God's relationship to His people. It is also a human story. We cannot help but admire Hosea's unflinching dedication to God's purpose. No matter how difficult the challenge, he was single-mindedly focused on doing the Lord's bidding, which was essentially to condemn the Israelites for their sinful and unfaithful ways. Needless to say, Hosea's message was not well received by his neighbors. His family most likely bore the brunt of their scorn. Hosea's wife, Gomer, had left him—and not for the first time.

As God persisted with his people, so Hosea went once more to recover his wayward wife. Why did she keep leaving Hosea? Was there anything left for the two of them to build a relationship on? In the end, do we choose love or does love choose us? All marriages have their ups and downs. Even the strongest and most loving of marriages face difficult challenges. In some ways, pastors and their wives and children carry the extra burden of higher expectations and less support than many other families. One can only imagine the pressure a prophet like Hosea and his family had to respond to in Old Testament times. And the fact that he selected his wife from a brothel and gave his children names only a masochist could appreciate made matters worse.

Hosea was a man driven by God's leading, and the news he brought to his people wasn't good. Needless to say, he, his wife, and his children weren't at the top of the community's summer barbeque invitation lists. There were whispers and jokes about Gomer's past and Hosea's children's present, like, "The apple doesn't fall far from the tree." Of course, Gomer fueled the fire with her escapades as well. She was the original runaway wife.

We don't really know what Hosea felt inside. We do know he was dedicated to God's call and that he used his family to illustrate his people's unfaithfulness to God's purpose and the consequences for such disobedience.

Still, marriage and children are more than an analogy or metaphor. They are flesh and bone, dirty diapers, and tears and laughter. Whatever it was for Hosea, it was apparently too much for Gomer. She kept running away and, to his credit, Hosea kept going after her. God only knows what their poor children were thinking about it all!

What we may learn from this story is that Hosea's persevering pursuit of Gomer in spite of her indiscretions is but a hint of God's patient, relentless pursuit of us. And as far as all the Gomers in our lives are concerned, loving God is only as effective as our ability and willingness to translate and demonstrate that affection to those closest to us.

QUESTIONS

1. How would you have reacted if God told you to go to a brothel to choose a wife and then have children with her, giving them names condemning Israel's disobedience? That would be like you and me naming our child Judas, Caiaphas, or Satan.

2. If you were Gomer, what do you think family life would be like if you were married to Hosea?

3. What if you were one of Hosea and Gomer's children? What would school be like? What about peer pressure?

4. In the story, what was the turning point for Gomer? What touched her and made her consider that there was room in Hosea's heart for God and her?

NOTES:

_____

_____

_____

_____

_____

_____

_____

_____

_____

_____

Interview with Joab

_____

_____

_____

_____

_____

4

LONG SHOT

LORD EDESH SAT with his arms folded across his chest and stared intently at Jareth, his captain. "What's your assessment of Saul's army?"

Jareth motioned for a man standing with his officers to come forward.

"Heber is one of Saul's soldiers who has come over to our side. We have interrogated him and believe the information he brings us is of value."

Lord Edesh motioned for a servant to pour a goblet of wine for the Israelite.

"What news do you bring us?"

Heber, the Israelite, gulped the wine quickly, wiping his mouth with the back of his hand.

"Many of us are afraid, and there is talk of desertion. A dark mood has come upon our king. He rarely leaves his tent."

"How many men are you talking about?"

"More than two dozen have already slipped away. I have also overheard some of the officers talk of returning to their homes."

Lord Edesh dismissed the Israelite with a wave of his hand and turned to his captain.

"Is this another Israelite trick or is the whole army ready to fold?"

Jareth leaned forward on his stool. "We both know that Saul is not the same man he once was. Our spies inform us that he is often taken by too much drink and worry. His doubt infects many of his officers and soldiers. It seems clear that the Israelite king who defeated the Ammonites is but a shadow of the warrior he once was."

"We should be grateful to our great god, Dagon, that Saul is king and not his son, Jonathan," Lord Edesh replied. "Ever since the prophet Samuel abandoned him, he has become predictably complacent."

"Yes," Jareth agreed, "our informers tell us that even with the Israelite victory at Michmash, Saul was reluctant to take advantage. Where Jonathan is bold, Saul is tentative. There is also talk of his jealousy regarding his son's leadership and initiative—to the point of ordering Jonathan's death for disobeying a meaningless order. Had it not been for a large outpouring of support among the people, many believe that Saul would have carried out his order of execution."

Lord Edesh rose from his chair and motioned for Jareth to do the same.

"It's a shame that we can't get Saul's son to come over to our side. We could use a man like him."

Jareth laughed. "True enough, Lord Edesh. But then, we do have Goliath."

With a clap from his hands, servants responded to Lord Edesh by bringing in platters of pork and vegetables, along with fresh-baked bread and jars of wine.

"Tomorrow will be decisive. Forty days is long enough. Saul and his rag-tag army are as ready to be delivered to us as is this platter of roasted pork we are about to eat."

It was a warmer morning than usual for that time of year. The young armor bearer handed Goliath his helmet.

"Are you ready, sir?"

"Yes," the massive warrior replied, placing the bronze helmet on his head. Goliath had fought a hundred or more such battles since his youth. Well-muscled and standing more than nine feet tall, he was an impressive specimen of war. He wore a coat of bronze scale armor and bronze greaves that protected his legs below the knees. A javelin was slung on his back.

Goliath rose from his stool and walked to the door of his tent, peering out into the morning mist. Lord Edesh of the Philistines had been a hard taskmaster, but the rewards had been substantial—a coastal estate worthy of a champion's stature and a wife, children, and servants. The fruits of his victories lay waiting within his grasp. He could almost smell the sea.

Goliath reached out his hand and his armor bearer, Rebath, poured wine into a cup and handed it to him.

It hadn't been an easy profession. He had the battle scars to prove it. And there had been several close calls, like the Amalekite warrior Nabosh who had tripped him with the staff of a spear and plunged a dagger deep into his left shoulder. Though he prevailed and the wound had healed, it still ached when the winter winds came.

Goliath was tired. He could feel it in his bones and the headaches he often experienced before battle. One more victory, and home and hearth would be his to enjoy. Lord Edesh had promised.

Goliath smiled as he drank the last of the wine.

"Let's go see Lord Edesh." He stood to his full height of nine feet and left his tent, with Rebath following close behind.

Long Shot

Lord Edesh stood talking with his advisors when Goliath entered his tent. Looking up from his war map, he grinned. "Is my champion ready for a great victory?"

Goliath bowed his head in agreement.

"Our priests have fasted and prayed through the night. Dagon has revealed to them that today you will be triumphant."

The priests of Dagon nodded solemnly as Edesh continued.

"Our forefathers claimed the southern coast of Canaan. The sea is in our blood. We have come out of Egypt and reclaimed our cities by the sea—Gaza, Ashkelon, Ashdod, Ekron, and Gath. We are strong like the iron points of our spears. Saul, their king, has lost his nerve. Today we defeat him, and with his defeat, the Israelites are ours."

As his priests voiced their support, Lord Edesh grew bolder.

"I want their 'Ark' back! We had it once before, but because our will was weak, Dagon abandoned us. Today he smiles upon us once more. Victory will be ours!"

The tent of Edesh reverberated with a loud chorus praising Dagon, their lord, and their bright, shining, undefeated champion, Goliath.

Goliath had heard it all before. He raised his cup and voice with all the others, letting their shouts of encouragement calm the nagging fear that always accompanied him into battle.

The mists had departed and the sun blazed down upon the battle lines in the Elah Valley as Goliath made his way toward the Israelites, Rebath walking before him carrying his shield. The hint of fear and the subtle throbbing in his head helped him focus on the task at hand.

"Why do you men of Israel line up for battle, yet send no one forth to challenge me?" Goliath shouted to them. "Is there not a man among you willing to fight for Saul, your king? Are you men, or women? I have come forth each day for the last forty, and yet today, as with all the other days, you women of Israel tremble in fear!"

As he had done in previous days, Goliath walked back and forth between the battle lines, taunting the Israelites. The demoralized soldiers of King Saul whispered among themselves and cast uneasy glances toward the giant that stood before them.

A lone figure emerged from their midst as Goliath finished his latest rant. He knelt and selected five smooth stones and put them in a pouch slung across his shoulder. He took a quick drink from the stream before rising to face the Philistine warrior.

Goliath squinted his eyes to see the figure more clearly. It was just a boy.

"And who is this?" roared Goliath. "Who is this child sent to do a man's job?"

"I am David, son of Jesse," the young boy replied with all the force he could muster.

Goliath and Rebath looked at each other incredulously, puzzled by the sight of the boy standing before them.

Goliath turned his attention once more to the Israelites. "Have you no shame? I have sons no older than this child. You have no warrior willing to fight me, but instead send this young boy as a sacrifice. Where, I ask you, is Saul hiding? Where is the coward who calls himself your king?"

Growing bolder, the shepherd boy replied in a clear, strong voice, "I come in the name of the Lord!"

A brief flash of Goliath's youngest son, full of bravado like the boy standing before him, quickly disappeared into the cold, hard reality of the task that was at hand.

Goliath's patience had run out. Killing children was not his preference, but the boy standing before him was an insult to his status as a champion, and as a man. Goliath could feel the anger and frustration welling up inside him.

Glaring at David, Goliath pointed his spear at the boy and bellowed, "Am I a dog that you come to fight me with a stick? Come closer and I'll feed your flesh to the birds."

The boy stood his ground and retorted with a voice that seemed much louder than it should have been, "This day the Lord of Israel will hand you over to me. I will kill you and cut off your head!"

"Enough," Goliath said to his armor bearer. "Let's get this over with."

As the Philistine champion approached, David reached into his pouch and loaded his sling with a single smooth stone.

Goliath hurled his spear, narrowly missing his intended target as David darted to his left. Crouching low to the ground, David began swinging his sling above his head in a wide arc.

As Goliath approached the crouching boy with sword in hand, he had an inclination to laugh, if only the sight were not so pathetic. "The die has been cast—get it over with," he muttered to himself as he raised his sword. "Just a few more moments—"

Goliath was confused by a stinging sensation that felt like the bite of an insect. His head hurt more than it normally did—a deep, piercing ache. It should have disappeared by now. He was having trouble with his vision. And he wondered why he was lying on his back.

Goliath squinted into the sun above him, trying to clear his head. Images flooded his fading consciousness. An early morning sea breeze and the smell of salt in the air. Laughing children. The look in his wife's eye on a warm summer's evening. His grandmother peeling fresh figs.

Long Shot

Goliath felt someone's foot on his chest. Who was the raised shadow above him?

Darkness.

COMMENTS

1 Samuel 17:1-58

We all know the story about how David, the shepherd boy, slew the Philistine giant, Goliath, with a slingshot and a few smooth stones. In a sense, David was Luke Skywalker before *Star Wars* was cool. The young hero brought down the giant villain and all was well—at least for a while.

But what about the villain? Wasn't Goliath also human? What if Goliath could tell us how he felt about being trotted out time and again to do his king's bidding? While looking through Goliath's eyes doesn't change the story's ending or the miracle of David's feat in serving God's purpose, it tempers the event within a human context.

Even in today's world, when we celebrate the demise or death of villains who threaten our own kind, it is too easy to forget that no matter how misguided they may have been, they were still human. Can we still feel a hint of sorrow or sadness that things could have turned out different for them? Can bad people change, as Saul did on the road to Damascus, or, for that matter, can good people do bad things, as David did after he became king?

Things are never exactly as they seem. Like Goliath and the Philistines, size, strength, and power do not always rule the day. Sometimes long shots come in.

If you were a betting person, you would have placed your bet on Goliath. The Philistines had superior weapons and an undefeated giant of a champion. The Israelites were afraid. Saul, their king, was uncertain and indecisive. Yet a young shepherd boy was willing to face what seemed to be insurmountable odds. What did he have that the king didn't?

Courage, sacrifice, and serving a higher purpose were among several traits David possessed that Saul apparently didn't. It would be a mistake to assume that David wasn't afraid. One can imagine his knees shaking as he faced Goliath. Courage is not the absence of fear, but doing what needs to be done in the face of such trepidation.

Two themes relevant to our lives are worth considering in this story. First, when we feel powerful and overconfident as Goliath did, we are often at our most vulnerable. Pride is not a virtue but a vice, and often a lethal one at that. Think of the mighty throughout history, who, riding the wave of military, corporate, athletic, and other kinds of success, have come to think of themselves as invincible, only to find themselves and those they represent in ruins. Skills fade and eventually abilities decline. A champion never stays number one for long, and what time brings, time takes away.

Second, when we feel overwhelmed, vulnerable, and helpless, we are often most open to change—to trying a new way of doing something. When we are most down, we are most apt to look up to a greater truth and reality.

It is easier for God to get the attention of modern-day Davids than Goliaths. When Goliaths fall, Davids rise. It is also worth noting that modern-day champions like Goliath in sports, politics, and commerce often become prisoners of their own success and celebrity, and end up being used by others for ill-gotten gains.

QUESTIONS

1. Can you think of historical examples of world leaders who, like Lord Edesh and Goliath, thought they were invincible and beyond the reach of justice?

2. What about the "Goliaths" of the corporate world like Enron? What lessons can be learned where tension exists between profits and ethics?

3. Can you think of champions who have gotten caught up in the hyped celebrity of their fame and image, only to be used by others in their fall from grace?

4. Can you think of examples of ordinary people who have shown extraordinary courage in facing overwhelming odds to save the day in one way or another?

5. What about personal examples in your own life where, like Goliath, pride and the expectations of others have led you down the path to disappointment? And when, like David, you felt small and disadvantaged, God lifted you back onto your feet and accomplished more through you in both big and small ways than you could have ever accomplished on your own?

NOTES:

_____

_____

_____

_____

_____

_____

_____

Long Shot

5

INTERVIEW WITH JOAB

H E STOOD AND watched the lone figure slowly make his way up the dusty path to his home. Although age had begun to overtake him, he was still a man to be reckoned with. He stood erect. There was an aura of strength and cunning about him, and his muscular arms bore several battle scars. Dark, piercing brown eyes tinged with a hint of gray peered out from a tanned, deeply lined face framed by a carefully manicured salt and pepper beard. Joab was a man well acquainted with difficult times and tasks. He stroked his beard and waited for the approaching visitor to arrive.

A servant entered the room. "Master, Nabeth, assistant to the king's historian, Jehoshaphat, has arrived."

After the two men greeted each other, one of Joab's servants placed a basin of water before the guest so that he could wash off some of the dust and grime of his journey. The servant then removed Nabeth's sandals and washed and dried his feet. Another servant entered with two jars, one filled with water, the other filled with wine. After filling both men's cups, she spread broiled fish and cakes of raisins and figs before them.

Joab motioned for the servants to leave them alone.

"Thank you for coming, Nabeth."

Nabeth nodded. "Jehoshaphat could not come. His duties have increased since Solomon was anointed by the priest Zadok and declared king."

Joab's mouth turned into a slow, crinkled smile. "I understand. My old friend Jehoshaphat must take care that he doesn't give the king the wrong impression. I'm no longer an asset to him, only a liability. But what about you, Nabeth? Aren't you concerned there will be whispers in Solomon's court regarding your visit to me?"

Nabeth reached for a fig. "I have known you and my old teacher, Abiathar, for many years. You have always been kind to my family. My brother, Geth, fought with you against the Philistines and the Amakelites and holds you in high regard to this day."

"Geth was a brave warrior," Joab replied. "Be sure to give him my regards the next time you see him. Do you know why I summoned Jehoshaphat?"

Interview with Joab

Breaking off some raisins, Nabeth viewed his host with some caution. "My guess is that with all the talk going around, you want there to be some sort of record of your side of the events."

Joab stroked his beard. "I have heard the rumors discrediting me, as I am sure you have. While I don't lay claim to an unblemished life, I want there to be a record of my motives or as you put it, 'my side of the story,' in the lifetime of service I have rendered to David and the kingdom of Israel and Judah." Joab drank deeply from his cup. "Time is short."

"You could flee."

Joab set his cup down and wiped his mouth with the back of his hand. "Too old…and too proud."

Nabeth looked up from his food. "And perhaps too many enemies?"

Joab shrugged. "Yes, that too." Joab's eyes burned. "I should have known better than to back Adonijah over Solomon. My brother Abishai stayed out of it. Foresight has never been one of my strong points. I'm a pragmatist. I do what has to be done. I suppose my brother is shrewder than I. All I knew was that Israel needed a king. And David, for all practical purposes, had retired from his duties. Unless, you consider laying with Abishag, the Shunammite woman, the only duty needed to run a kingdom."

"Even so, and I mean no disrespect," Nabeth replied as he wiped his hands on a towel, "backing Adonijah over Solomon, whose mother, Bathsheba, many feel was David's favorite wife, was a bold and, some say, even reckless move."

Joab's eyes blazed with resentment. "To hell with Bathsheba and Solomon. A good man died because of her. Uriah the Hittite was a fine captain. They didn't come any braver or more loyal."

Nabeth looked puzzled. "But didn't King David summon her to him? How could she refuse? And didn't you—"

The dark burning look from Joab stopped Nabeth in mid-sentence.

Joab drained his cup and stared into the bottom of it, talking as much to himself as his visitor. "I know what I did—better than you or anyone else can imagine. I know there is blood on my hands—David's as well. More than once I did the dirty work that had to be done for my king, not that he ever truly appreciated it. I have lived with the regret of my actions regarding Uriah. Still, what I did doesn't excuse Bathsheba. Some say she knew what she was doing—that she wanted to catch the eye of David. She wouldn't be the first."

"Many others believe she was innocent of any intrigue. Helpless before the power and charm of the king," Nabeth countered.

Joab grunted his disagreement.

Growing bolder, Nabeth asked, "Why Adonijah? Why the brother of Absalom? They seemed so much alike—charming, handsome, vain, and dangerously naive."

Clapping his hands, Joab ordered the servants to bring more wine. He thought carefully before answering Nabeth's query.

"Your question is a good one. You could say I should have known better, and of course in hindsight, you would be right. But when the priest Abiathar discussed the state of the kingdom with me, it boiled down to Adonijah or Solomon—a man or a boy."

"Why not Solomon?" Nabeth interjected. "He has demonstrated discernment and a certain mature wisdom even at his relatively young age—an ability to resolve disputes between disagreeable parties."

Joab popped a dried fig in his mouth, peering at Nabeth with a patient, yet frustrated look at his guest's lack of insight. "I'll give you that. Solomon is a clever lad, maybe even beyond his years regarding political astuteness, but a man he is not." Joab's eyes narrowed and his mood grew darker. "David killed Goliath when he was but a boy. I was there, serving as one of Jonathan's captains. What in God's name has Solomon done? What battlefield has he proven himself on? A Goliath can't be slain with clever words, even if your mother is the king's favorite." Joab leaned back against the coolness of the wall and wiped the sweat from his brow. "I'm well aware of Adonijah's limitations, as well as his strengths. He is, as you say, handsome, charming, and politically naive. And like his brother Absalom before him, politically ambitious—a potentially lethal combination. But unlike Absalom, he was willing to listen to those with more experience."

Nabeth flicked a fly away from his face. "If only Adonijah had not pushed his luck with Solomon."

"No doubt," Joab replied. "But like his brother Absalom before him, Adonijah couldn't leave well enough alone. His vanity and ambition did him in. Having Bathsheba forward his request to Solomon to give him Abishag, David's last concubine, for his wife, sealed Adonijah's fate. And my guess is that Bathsheba was only too happy to oblige the poor idiot's request."

Nabeth took a sip of wine. "Forgiveness once, but not a second time."

Joab nodded in agreement.

Nabeth continued. "Now Adonijah is no more, killed by the hand of Benaiah, head of the king's bodyguards."

"On the king's order," Joab added with the hint of a grimace. "And now that David has passed, I will be next."

"Perhaps there is hope," Nabeth replied. "Solomon spared Abiathar. He dismissed him from the priesthood, but at least Solomon let him return to his home in peace."

Joab smiled wearily. "You know better, my young friend. Benaiah will also come for me and many others after me before his time is finished serving the new king." Joab looked out of the window into the sweltering midday heat. "I wonder if Benaiah has any idea what being the king's henchman means?"

"Means?" Nabeth asked.

Joab turned a tired, steady gaze from the window to his guest.

"Benaiah has become Solomon's Joab. He will do for Solomon what I did for his father before him."

"But Abiathar was spared a—"

Joab interrupted Nabeth again. "Abiathar was a priest, not a warrior. We were both, in our own way, loyal to David, but a priest has a better chance of keeping his head. Abiathar is one who suggests; I am one who takes action. His bloodstains are hidden, mine more apparent."

Joab and Nabeth grew silent once more.

Finally Joab rose to his feet. "The heat of the day tires me. We can continue our conversation after we rest, if you, my young friend, will stay the night."

Nabeth agreed to his host's request and Joab called for the servants.

―――――

The cool of the evening found Joab and Nabeth sitting in the courtyard under a pomegranate tree.

"The roasted lamb is excellent," Nabeth said, licking his fingers.

Joab folded his arms across his chest. "Only the best for Jehoshaphat's assistant."

Nabeth smiled and wiped his hands on a towel the servants had provided him. "I'm curious. You said you saw David slay Goliath. What was it like?"

As Joab smoothed a wrinkle out of his tunic, it was clear to Nabeth that Joab relished the memory.

"How can one describe such an event? Like the rising of the sun after a black, starless night. Or the illumination of a full moon on the last night of a desperate harvest. A boy with a slingshot against a champion the caliber of Goliath? It seemed like a miracle. We all felt a glimmer of hope again. Simple as that."

"You sound like a poet," Nabeth smiled.

Joab's pleasant remembrance disappeared. "No poet. Just a magic moment pointing toward a better future. Those days are gone."

Nabeth reached for the wineskin. "Those were amazing times. Not for Saul, but for David and Israel."

Joab shrugged. "Saul wasn't a bad fellow. Back then the Philistines were always at us, and they often had the upper hand, at that. I admired Saul's courage. He was brave but not as smart as his oldest son, Jonathan. Now

Jonathan was a leader of men, not brooding like his father. Where Saul was impatient, Jonathan was careful. When Saul grew afraid, Jonathan knew how to be bold when the right time came—like the time at the cliff near Micmash when he and his armor bearer killed twenty Philistines. Where Saul and any normal man who was a prince or king would feel threatened by the likes of David, Jonathan wasn't. He accepted David—loved him like a brother. Even protected him from his father."

"After that, Saul got on the bad side of the prophet Samuel," Nabeth interjected.

"Like I said, Saul was a man of contradictions. He could be a brave, fierce warrior, then turn around and fall into one of his moods and become fearful and indecisive. Saul wasn't a natural leader. Too prone to changing his mind. And of course, like all kings, more than a little vain."

"Aren't we all, to one degree or another, men of contradictions and each in our own way given to vanity?" countered Nabeth.

"True enough," grunted Joab. "You sound more like a priest than a historian."

Nabeth chuckled at the thought. "Was it the monument to himself that Saul set up at Carmel or the times he didn't obey Samuel's instructions that did him in?"

"Maybe all of it. The one that stands out to me was when Saul spared the Amalekite king, Agag, contrary to Samuel's instructions. I never saw Samuel so mad. Old Agag thought he was safe until he felt the point of that old prophet's dagger in his belly."

Joab tore off a small piece of bread and began to chew.

"Things were never the same after that between Saul and Samuel. That was the beginning of the end for Saul."

"Yes," Nabeth mused. "Kings may speak for the people, but the prophet speaks for God. The one in the end always seems to trump the other."

"Like Nathan," Joab spat.

"Yes, like Nathan," Nabeth agreed, taking a small sip of wine.

Joab looked hard at Nabeth. "You may be right, but like I said earlier, I'm a realist who does what has to be done right here and now in this world. And what has to be done isn't always a pretty sight. You say Samuel and Nathan speak for God. Maybe so, but not ever having heard God speak, my take on their actions is that they either want more power and influence or at least keep what they have. That's something I understand. A man ought to take responsibility for his ambitions and not blame it on God."

Nabeth pensively rubbed his chin. "Yet Nathan did call David to account for his adulterous affair and having Uriah placed in a position of battle that was sure to result in his death."

"No need to remind me of that," Joab snorted, "or my role in it. The death of Uriah is but one of many burdens I carry."

"I'm sorry."

"No need to apologize either," Joab continued. "What you say is true. Nathan did call David out about his transgression. It is also true that Nathan now conspires with Bathsheba, and with the help of the priest Zadok has seen that her son, Solomon, has been anointed king. Nathan has gone from public condemnation of David and Bathsheba's affair to public affirmation of Bathsheba and her son." Joab looked at Nabeth with a wry grin. "I know, I know. Poor Bathsheba had no choice in the matter. She was as innocent as a lamb. I guess the Lord does work in mysterious ways."

"Back to Saul for a moment, if you don't mind," Nabeth suggested. "My understanding is that he didn't always feel threatened by David."

Joab refilled his cup with wine. "As I said earlier, Saul was a troubled, somewhat unpredictable man. His dark moods could last for days. During those times, nothing could lift Saul's spirits like David's harp. We were always relieved when David played because that meant the king's mood would improve, and things would get done."

Nabeth pulled a cloak around his shoulders to ward off the chill of the night air.

"But that was before Goliath?"

"For the most part," Joab replied. "After Goliath, everything began to change." Joab chuckled to himself. "Who would have ever thought that a young sheep-herding harp player would kill a warrior like Goliath with a slingshot…and then bring down a king?"

"Like you said, General, the Lord works in mysterious ways," Nabeth said, pulling his cloak tighter.

Joab looked at the shadows from the lamplight dancing along the wall surrounding his home. "Perhaps so. Perhaps so. One thing is for certain—that time was one of the lowest points in my and many of the other soldiers' lives. The Philistines were taunting us, and our king was paralyzed with a fear that infected us all. A young sheep-herder displayed courage that none of the rest of us possessed."

"It has been rumored that you wanted to press the attack against the Philistines but were forbidden to do so."

Joab shrugged. "I was only a commander of fifty in Jonathan's army. I was scared like the rest, but after forty days of humiliation, my anger and shame was greater than my fear. Still, I was afraid and didn't press the issue with Jonathan. Truth is, he was more eager to attack than I was. I'm ashamed to say so, but I was ready to run for my life like the rest."

"Still," Nabeth exclaimed, "that had to be great day! The power of Jehovah—to take a shepherd's son, a mere boy, and defeat a great warrior like

Goliath!"

Joab nodded. "Like I said, it was the greatest of days. And in a way, perhaps the worst of days as well."

Nabeth looked slightly confused. "What do you mean?"

"I mean it took a boy to do a man's job. David with his slingshot showed what a sorry state the rest of our army was in. He accepted a warrior's challenge while we cowered in fear."

"But Jehovah delivered you and all of Israel," Nabeth countered. "Was it not a mighty miracle that demonstrated the power of our God?"

"Perhaps, but remember, my young friend, I am a soldier, not a prophet or even a priest. No matter how bright the light—and no light was brighter than David's on that day—there are always the shadows."

"Could not the brightness of that light also be the glory of Jehovah's might and deliverance?"

Joab thought for a moment. "I suppose so," he conceded, "but David, not Jehovah, is the one I saw."

"And what do you mean about there always being the shadows?" Nabeth queried.

Joab rubbed his hands together over the small fire his servants had made to warm him and his guest. "What I mean is that I am a realist, as I've said. I see what is in front of me. Where you see a miracle from above, I see a victory in battle. That bright moment you speak of that signaled David's rise also signaled Saul's descent."

Nabeth pushed his point. "You don't believe in the power of Jehovah?"

Joab looked at Nabeth. "I don't deny it."

"That's not what I asked," a perplexed Nabeth replied.

Joab leaned toward the fire. "Let me put it this way. David loved the Lord God Jehovah. I loved David."

"Like Jonathan?"

A small smile creased Joab's face. "No, not like Jonathan. David and Jonathan were alike in so many ways—natural leaders, courageous and politically adept. They were the same, yet different: Jonathan, the polished prince, son of a king; David, the son of a farmer and herdsman, unpolished but still discerning and naturally charismatic. Jonathan was willing to risk everything to protect David, which of course made his father, Saul, furious."

"After David's victory over Goliath, Saul began to turn on David," Nabeth asserted.

"Yes, it's well known," Joab replied. "Everyone could see it coming. The one who soothed Saul's fears became the greatest source of his fear. And to a king who was often riddled with doubt and fear, that was the worst sort of torment."

Interview with Joab

Nabeth leaned toward Joab. "And the song, 'Saul has slain his thousands and David his tens of thousands' didn't help matters any."

"As you can imagine, it only made things worse." Joab took a sip of wine and placed another stick of wood on the fire. "As I have said, you and many others look at the defeat of Goliath as a great miracle. To me, if such things as miracles exist, the fact that David could survive Saul's jealousy and wrath is an even greater one. What are the odds that Jonathan, the king's son and heir, would protect his primary challenger to the throne? David was like a cat with nine lives. While those around him, like the priests of Nob, were slaughtered on Saul's order, David was always one step ahead of the king's sword."

Nabeth marveled at Joab's insight. "It doesn't really seem possible that David could have survived, unless you factor in divine providence—the will of Jehovah. Saul, like kings before him, did not take kindly to anyone who threatened his authority."

Joab poked the embers with a stick, watching sparks spiral into the darkness.

"With Saul, it was more than the threat of David taking his crown. The king was also a father. He loved Jonathan as his son and heir. And Jonathan was a worthy heir, not like Absalom, Adonijah, or Solomon. When a king's son, who has been raised to succeed him, loves another more than the one who sired and nurtured him, it is a hard thing to overcome. That is especially true when the heir apparent betrays his father, the king, in order to protect another who would be king—that is perhaps, the deepest wound of all."

"I never thought of that," Nabeth responded. "How difficult it must have been for Saul. Still, David had many chances to kill Saul, but never took advantage of his opportunities - like the incident at the desert of En Gedi."

"No, he didn't," Joab replied. "I encouraged David to attack Saul and his men at En Gedi and be done with it, but he would not agree to my plan."

"Why not? Why would David continue to spare one who hounded and pursued him with no good end in mind?"

Joab stared at the crackling fire.

"While Saul feared and even hated David, he also admired him. Likewise, even though David feared Saul's wrath, he admired and even loved him. More importantly, he didn't want to kill the Lord's anointed. David was strange in that way. He took the prophets seriously, not just as a political tool, but as those he believed spoke for God. In matters of war and politics, David bowed to the will of Jehovah. In matters of the flesh…well, that was another story."

Nabeth rubbed his hands together over the fire. "Back to the incident at En Gedi. David sparing Saul's life while he slept seemed to change things somewhat."

Joab spat in the fire. "I suppose it did. Of course, Saul wouldn't have done the same if he had found David sleeping. He would have cut off a lot more than the corner of David's robe. Anyway, Saul quit pursuing David when David went to live among the Philistines. How ironic is that?"

"Yes," Nabeth replied. "The enemy of Israel becomes the protector of the one who killed their champion. Then when the Witch of Endor summoned the spirit of Samuel who gave the bad news to Saul—"

"That was the last straw," Joab interrupted. "Saul was doomed. He died by his own hand in the battle with the Philistines."

"Still, David mourned the deaths of Saul and Jonathan," Nabeth continued.

"As I have already said," Joab grunted, "David both feared and admired Saul as God's anointed. And, of course, he loved Jonathan."

"Then you, Joab, came to power when David was anointed king of Judah," Nabeth replied, looking intently at the old warrior sitting across the fire from him.

"I suppose so," Joab said as much to himself as to Nabeth. "Those were difficult times. Abner, the general of Saul's armies, tried to prop up Ish-Bosheth, the weakest of Saul's sons as king of Israel. Abner was the real power. Ish-Bosheth was no more than a puppet who thought the only requirement to be king was to be born in a royal household. Then, when the best of Abner's chosen warriors were defeated by the twelve soldiers we chose, all hell broke loose."

"Wasn't that when Abner killed your brother Asahel?"

Joab's mood grew noticeably darker. "Yes, Asahel was killed by Abner's own hand."

Nabeth stared at Joab. "Some say that although Abner warned Asahel, your brother continued his relentless pursuit of him."

Joab spat once again into the fire, making a hissing sound.

"It was war."

"Still, Abner did in the end deliver Israel to David, and as a result, David sent him away in peace."

Joab scowled at Nabeth. "Maybe peace with David, but not peace with me and my brother Abishai. The sons of Zeruiah spill the blood of those who spill ours. We avenge those who bring harm to our family."

"Your actions didn't please David," Nabeth replied as delicately as possible.

Joab grunted. "He gave Abner honor he didn't deserve, and by doing that, pointed the finger at me. The soldiers under my command didn't know what to think."

Interview with Joab

"Perhaps, it was a political necessity in uniting the kingdom," Nabeth offered as an explanation.

"Political necessity or not, Abner was a threat. He was the enemy, clear and simple. His purpose was to overthrow David, and I told the king as much. Even if he hadn't killed Asahel, Abner would have been a threat whether David believed it or not."

Nabeth refilled Joab's cup from the wineskin. "And perhaps a threat to you as well?'

Joab glared at him but said nothing.

The two men sat in silence until Nabeth finally spoke.

"There were some good days after that, it seems. The Ark of the Covenant was brought to Jerusalem—a time of great celebration."

Joab ran his hands through his hair, looking past Nabeth into the night sky. "Yes, there was a period of prosperity and celebration. We defeated everyone who stood before us—the Moabites, Ammonites, Philistines and a host of others. I admired David for his courage and spirit in battle—and for his generosity with me and the soldiers who served him. Still, what goes up must come down. The young shepherd boy with a slingshot who so inspired us became king and played psalms with his harp. But his harp also played to the wine-soaked pleasures of an endless parade of concubines. Then came Bathsheba, and his sons who he spoiled with abandon. They knew nothing of his humble origins except as legend. They preened, pranced, and postured their way around the court, currying favor and intrigue wherever they could find it, while their father the king ignored their shortcomings and exaggerated their limited gifts and abilities."

Nabeth nodded. "And then came Absalom."

The pain in Joab's weathered face was real and apparent, unlike any expression Nabeth had observed during his visit with the old warrior and commander.

Joab poured more wine. "Absalom favored his father in a number of ways—handsome, charismatic—but where David was brave and passionate, Absalom was cunning and calculating. The two were often at odds with each other about one thing or another, and everything got worse over time. And when he was younger, I took an interest in Absalom's progress as a warrior. He was a quick and eager student of those arts. I tried to clean up the mess between him and his father when I realized what Absalom was up to. But as I have told you, diplomacy is not one of my strengths."

Nabeth warmed his hands over the small fire as he responded. "Their relationship continued to deteriorate."

"Yes," Joab replied. "As Absalom's popularity and conspiracy continued to grow, David ignored the obvious."

Nabeth looked at Joab across the fire. "Kings have been known to become complacent—to take their kingdoms for granted."

His voice rising, Joab pointed at Nabeth for emphasis. "When they do, they do so at their own peril. I tried to warn David, but he would have none of it!"

The two men grew silent once more, listening to the crackling fire.

Finally, Joab spoke. "My proud, victorious king fled Jerusalem like a dog with his tail between his legs, afraid of his own son."

"Many thought Absalom would be victorious," Nabeth mused, "especially with a charismatic commander like Amasa to lead his army. Everything seemed to be in place for certain victory."

"Amasa," Joab spat. "More clever in the rhetoric of politics than the art of war. In the forest of Ephraim, our swords, spears, and arrows did the talking. The counselor Hushai's advice played to Absalom's vanity and ambition, and we closed the trap."

Nabeth responded in a hushed voice. "You won the battle, but broke the father's heart."

Joab's eyes burned with pain and anger. "I did what had to be done. My loyalty to David demanded no less. I would have preferred another way, but a broken heart is better than a dead king."

Nabeth contemplated the fire's burning embers. "It must have been difficult when you met with David. What you said to him has been repeated often: 'You love those who hate you and hate those who love you.'"

Joab's shoulders sagged. "The men who had fought and bled for him were confused and disheartened by his mourning for Absalom. I had to do something."

"It worked," Nabeth replied. "David went to his soldiers and thanked them for their loyalty and sacrifice."

Joab frowned. "It worked, but at a heavy price."

"What price?"

"I killed the beloved son of the king. When I killed Absalom, a part of David died—along with any feeling he had for me." Joab stared at the fire. "I crossed a line that had to be crossed, but a grieving father sees only the sorrow of his loss with no appreciation of what was saved."

"David showed his displeasure by appointing Amasa commander-in-chief of the army," Nabeth replied.

Joab began to slowly rock back and forth. "It was Abner all over again, only worse. Forgiving such a threat only encourages an even greater catastrophe."

"Perhaps," Nabeth responded, "but when you and your brother Abishai killed Amasa, David did reinstate you as commander-in-chief of his army."

"He needed me. That's all," Joab replied. "He needed someone who would do what had to be done."

Nabeth cast a quizzical glance at Joab. "After killing Amasa and bringing him the head of Sheba, perhaps David feared you—even if just a little."

Joab folded his hands in his lap and looked intently at him. "Perhaps, but it is of little matter now, my young friend. Soon Benaiah and Solomon's bodyguard will come for me. It is enough that you have heard me speak of my life with David so that when others recount past victories and events, there will be a record of Joab's account."

Nabeth returned Joab's gaze. "What will you do when they come?"

"I will die," Joab replied with a weary smile. "I will take sanctuary and cling to the horns of the altar, and hope for mercy from Solomon that is not likely to come."

"You do not look afraid."

Joab's smile disappeared. He looked his age, an old man worn out and scarred by years of battle and intrigue. "I am afraid. If you look closely, you will see fear in my eyes. Still, I will wait for Benaiah to come and do what has to be done—as I always have."

COMMENTS

2 Samuel: 2-24; 1 Kings 1-2:34

For many years, Joab was King David's right-hand man, often doing the dirty work behind the scenes—cleaning up mistakes David made and keeping the kingdom running.

Like most "enforcers" throughout history, Joab ended up with blood on his hands and a list of enemies that stretched around the block. Solomon, upon David's death, took his father's advice and sent his own enforcer to "clean up" Joab.

We have all heard the saying in one form or another about how power corrupts and that absolute power corrupts absolutely. David went from being a nondescript young shepherd boy to the hero of Israel in short order with only a slingshot and a few smooth stones. From that point on, his rise to power, though fraught with danger at times, seemed inevitable. From the innocent shepherd boy who slew the giant to the celebrity king who had one of his loyal officers killed so he could take the man's wife, Bathsheba, for his own, David struggled to keep his shepherd's heart as a check and balance to his king's ego—often unsuccessfully.

During a debate once, one party suggested that one could be both a shepherd and king. The opposing party responded with a thoughtful question: when was David closest to God, when he was the shepherd boy or the king? Like all kings and political leaders, it seems easier to maintain one's virtue before ascending the throne or taking office than after one has settled into the challenges and privilege of rule and governance. The call for compromise is endless—some of it good and some of it destructive—as is the temptations of power. Throughout David's reign, his right-hand man and primary "enabler" was often Joab, in public and, perhaps even more often, in private.

Joab was not a handshaking, back-slapping politician. He had none of David's charm and charisma. His instrument was more the sword than the harp. Laughter didn't come easily to him, and grudges were not easily forgotten or forgiven. He was more comfortable in the shadows, watching and observing, often with suspicion, the intentions and behavior of those with whom King David came into contact. Joab wanted to be a "mover and shaker," and he got his wish, so to speak, but at a heavy price in the end. He probably received more than his share of the spoils of victory, but while the king basked in the limelight, Joab often stayed busy taking care of loose ends and cleaning up the messes David had made behind the scenes. In enabling David's excesses, Joab became inextricably entwined in the consequences of the king's poor choices. With constant intrigue comes a certain amount of paranoia, to which Joab was no stranger. Deceit, betrayal, ambush, even killing Absalom contrary to David's wishes became Joab's price of admission to the seat of power. In killing Absalom to protect David, Joab crossed a line with the king that could never be repaired. From Joab's perspective, he was in a no-win situation, yet he willingly crossed a line from which he couldn't return.

There is no evidence that Joab started out corrupt. He may have been a somewhat ill-tempered and curmudgeonly soldier, but his skills as a military leader and his loyalty to David seem apparent. Moving from the company of soldiers in the field to the king's palace required a kind of metamorphosis that perhaps Joab desired but was not especially well suited for.

If there are any lessons to be learned in this story, they seem to be twofold. While we need good, courageous role models, beware of heroes when they become celebrities. As the old saying goes, "All that glitters is not gold." Even a man or a king after God's own heart still has a shadowy side and feet of clay.

Also, we may ask ourselves if we are enablers or encouragers with our friends and families. Do we primarily "clean up messes" or do we encourage those we care about to grow up and accept responsibility for their choices? While we need positive, moral and spiritually mature persons in positions of power and leadership, regardless of the setting, we should pay close attention to what an invitation to power may cost. What good is it if costs us our soul?

QUESTIONS

1. What do you think happened to David and Joab? Why and how did they evolve from who they were in the beginning to who they became at the end of their lives?

2. What were Joab's strengths and weaknesses? How was he an "enabler"? What do you think his relationship to God was?

3. In what ways may you and I be like Joab and David? At what point in our lives do we most depend on God's guidance?

4. In a way Joab, like many of us, served two masters. While at times his actions may have served God's purposes, his loyalty seemed more oriented toward David and his own self-interests. Can that be true for us as well, whether our master might be a person we admire and believe in or a desire for wealth, fame and power?

5. Should we become lost like Joab, is there a way back? What will it cost us to find our way back? How can we return to a shepherd's heart?

NOTES:

_____

_____

_____

_____

_____

_____

_____

_____

Interview with Joab

_____

_____

_____

_____

_____

_____

_____

6

THE OTHER SIDE OF THE ROAD

Two young boys chased a third past an outdoor table on a Jerusalem side street in the mid-afternoon sun. Their playful shouts grew faint as two men sitting next to the table watched them disappear in a trail of dust.

Jonas dipped a piece of bread in a small bowl of olive oil, while Timedechus, his companion, signaled to a rotund elderly man that their cups needed refilling.

"I'm not quite sure why we continue to patronize this place," Timedechus said. "Nathan's wine tastes more like water than wine, and his bread grows more stale with each visit!"

Jonas tore off another piece of bread. "Like I say each time you complain, it's convenient. Halfway between the tabernacle and the synagogue." Popping the piece of bread into his mouth, he smiled at the Levite. "Gives us more time to complain about the food and drink and offer our wise commentary on anything else that suits our fancy."

Timedechus chuckled. "Speaking of your expert opinion, what's your assessment of this year's Passover celebration, now that it has ended?"

Jonas held out his cup to be filled by a grumpy Nathan before replying. "All in all, it went well. A good turnout, and a number of excellent readings from the Scriptures."

Timedechus took a sip from his cup. "I have heard from several of your fellow priests that your reading and commentary from Exodus was one of the highlights."

Jonas smiled. "Spoken like a true friend. But I would have to say the most interesting highlight was the young boy's impromptu questions and responses to a group of priests on the last day of the festival. He was really quite dazzling."

Timedechus reached for an olive. "The lad was perhaps more an anomaly than a highlight. After all, he's just a carpenter's son. And from Nazareth at that. You know what they say about Nazareth...."

Jonas laughed. "Yes, I know. 'Nothing good ever comes out of Nazareth.'"

Timedechus continued. "There is no indication that the young boy has ever been mentored by a priest or rabbi of note. Some even suspect the boy simply memorized his comments to impress the elders. You know as well as I that Raboth, the priest assigned to Nazareth, is as ambitious as they come."

A donkey piled high with kindling brayed his complaint as his owner pulled on the overburdened animal's harness in an effort to move him forward.

Jonas took another swallow of wine. "I was there. I saw no sign of pretense with the boy, though he was precocious. And his parents were none too happy when they finally found him. Seems he got lost—perhaps on purpose—in the shuffle of their journey back to Nazareth. Besides, Raboth's not smart enough to conceive, let alone pull off, something like that. Raw ambition also requires ability to be successful."

Timedechus nodded in agreement. "That doesn't mean he won't try to take whatever credit he can for the young man's performance. Anything to impress the elders."

Jonas grew silent as he stroked his beard.

"What are you thinking, my friend?" Timedechus asked as he leaned back against the wall.

Jonas turned to his companion. "What do you make of this 'good Samaritan' everyone's talking about?"

Timedechus placed his hands on his knees. "I'll give even half-breed Samaritans credit where credit's due. He did a good thing. He gave aid to a Jew who had been beaten, robbed, and left for dead. Everyone knows the desert country outside of Jericho is a dangerous stretch of road. The authorities should provide more patrols."

Jonas continued to rub his beard. "Not only did he rescue him, but he spent several days' wages to ensure that the injured man was cared for. He went the extra mile. Some of the elders are saying the man is a hero, Samaritan or not."

Timedechus flicked a bread crumb off the sleeve of his tunic. "I don't know about him being a hero, but he did provide an act of compassion for a victim who was in need."

Staring off into space, Jonas said to Timedechus, "I was on the Jericho road that day."

The Levite smiled sheepishly. "Me too."

Jonas's eyes widened. "Did you see him?"

Timedechus nodded in affirmation. "I took a quick look but moved to the other side of the road and kept my distance. Like I said, that's a very dangerous stretch of road. More than one person has been lured into a fatal trap by stopping to aid someone who was only pretending to be injured while their fellow outlaws were hiding nearby."

Jonas shrugged his shoulders. "You're right, of course. I acted much the same way. I admit I was concerned about the man's well-being…but I was also a bit afraid. And to be completely honest, I was running late."

"For what?" Timedechus asked.

"I needed to prepare for the Sabbath service. A lot of people were depending on me."

Both men grew quiet.

Jonas coughed. He looked at Timedechus and cleared his throat. "I did include the man in my Sabbath prayers."

Timedechus rubbed his right knee. "You are a better man than me, Jonas, son of Ashmer. I did not even think to include him in my prayers. I assumed it was a setup. And I too was behind schedule. We Levites have a lot to do at Passover time." Timedechus reached over and patted Jonas gently on the shoulder. "It's not easy caring for the spiritual and religious needs of Israel. They are not an easy flock to guide. Sometimes we have to keep our eyes on the bigger picture—the greater good. And if I had known the man was really injured—that there was no trap—I believe I would have responded differently."

Jonas stared intently at his friend. "The Samaritan didn't know."

Timedechus raised his eyebrows and smiled. "The occasional 'good Samaritan' does not a virtuous tribe make. You are a priest, I am a Levite, and he, my friend, is still a Samaritan in spite of what a few of our more liberal elders might proclaim."

"Maybe so," Jonas replied as he rose from the bench. "But he stopped… and we kept walking."

COMMENTS

Luke 10:25-37

The story of the "Good Samaritan" offers us a timeless parable about help-ing those in need, especially those who are different from us or who we feel are beneath us in some way. People from Samaria were generally looked down upon by Israelites. Yet, it was a Samaritan who went the extra mile in offering aid to a victim wounded by bandits, while a Levite and a priest walked on by, making no effort to help.

We are all in a hurry. We would like to stop and help, but we have an ap-pointment to keep, so we say a little prayer instead of offering aid. A friend of mine once said that modern human beings have more labor and timesav-ing devices available to them than at any other time in history but, ironi-cally, have less free time than ever. Unlike us, the Levite and the priest in the story didn't have the technology and devices we enjoy, no cell phones or computers or cars. They walked to their destination and kept company with themselves or any companions who might happen to be traveling with them. In one sense, they weren't as easily distracted as we might be in today's world. While they may have been in a hurry, they weren't driving and talk-ing on a cell phone at the same time. They clearly saw the injured victim who had been beaten and robbed. They walked by like we drive by. Perhaps they even said a quick prayer.

On one level, we can imagine that the priest and the Levite might have been so committed to the "business" of religion that they had no time to be truly compassionate—to give a sip of cool water to one in need. Unlike Mother Teresa, they didn't see the injured victim as "Christ in a distressing disguise." We can also imagine on a deeper level that they, like we often are, were afraid—afraid that the victim was a decoy who might bring harm to them. Formality and fear often go together.

The least likely person, a Samaritan—considered to be unclean—was the one who stopped and offered generous compassion and care to the vic-tim. Not the true believers, but the one considered unworthy demonstrated the essence of what the priest and Levite claimed to stand for, but didn't act upon.

What does it take to touch the untouchable?

QUESTIONS

1. What did you think about the reasons the two friends gave for not stopping and helping the injured man?

2. How did religious and other kinds of prejudice keep them, and how does it keep us, from seeing others, whether they are the victims or persons who come to their aid, as being fully human?

3. Can you think of times when you were a victim of, if not a criminal assault, perhaps heartbreak? Can you remember occasions when a "Good Samaritan" came to your aid? When you were the Good Samaritan helping someone else?

4. Do you remember times when you "walked on by" and the regret you felt in not doing what you could have done to help? What can we learn from such experiences?

NOTES:

_____

_____

_____

_____

_____

_____

_____

_____

_____

7

ANOTHER PLACE

I N THE COOL of a late summer's evening, two men sat on a rock outcropping and watched the sheep graze below them.

Eliphaz took a long drink of water from the goat skin he carried looped over his shoulder.

"Your herd is growing."

Job nodded in agreement as he looked toward the horizon.

Eliphaz turned to Job. "I still regret my actions during your time of loss and suffering."

"You weren't alone," Job replied abruptly, continuing to gaze at a ridge of mountains in the distance.

"That may be true," Eliphaz sighed, "but I said what I said and did what I did. In your time of greatest need, I gave advice when you needed comfort. As your friend, I should have been changing your bandages. Instead, I offered you an explanation for your condition. I thought with my head when I should have felt with my heart. I let you down and two years later, it still bothers me."

Job shrugged. "What's past is past."

"That may be true," Eliphaz continued, "but good fortune today and even hope in the future doesn't always erase the burden of the past."

Job toyed with his beard and looked at Eliphaz out of the corner of his eye. "It doesn't have to. It just has to be enough."

"Enough what?"

"Enough to tip the balance. Enough to get up in the morning instead of staying in bed. Enough to look forward rather than backward—enough to bear in peace whatever the day brings you. Enough."

Eliphaz looked intently at Job. "I thank you again for tipping the balance for me and the others—for praying to God on our behalf. We didn't deserve your forgiveness."

Returning his gaze to the horizon, Job replied, "What choice is there—to forgive, or add even more grief and anger to a burden that's already heavy? If I ever really cared about you, how could I turn away from you in the end—even if you did add to my sorrows?"

Another Place

The two men returned to the silence of their own thoughts. Eliphaz offered his goatskin to Job, who drank deeply before handing it back to him. Eliphaz in turn, drank his fill. He plugged the goatskin and turned to Job once more.

"I've never seen faithfulness like yours. When covered with sores and after all that was taken from you, you said that even if God killed you, you would still love and trust Him. A part of me realized at that moment how small and weak my own faith was."

Job looked at Eliphaz but said nothing.

"At least your perseverance and faithfulness have been rewarded. You are now more prosperous than ever. More sheep, more oxen, more camels. Your wife pregnant again."

Job interrupted his friend with a look that unsettled Eliphaz.

"Be careful with your words, Eliphaz. While it is true that I am grateful for the Lord's blessing, my memory tempers whatever good fortune has come my way with past losses. I still remember the loss of my sons and daughters, their laughter, the light they brought into my life. They remain alive in my heart. How do I replace them? And how do I replace my wife's lost trust and rejection with the sweet innocence that came before it? You might also consider that as good as a friend's forgiveness feels both to the one who gives it and the one who receives it, the relationship is never quite the same as it was before. So yes, my friend, I have been blessed, but my gain is tempered in one way or another against what was lost."

The bleating of sheep echoed from below.

"Is there any constant in life?" Eliphaz asked.

"God is constant—the only constant."

Eliphaz rubbed his eyes. "And you met God—face to face. I know of no one else who has done so. What was it like? Where did it happen?"

Job took a deep breath before responding.

"Another place," he said finally.

"Another place?"

"Yes, another place. Not here, nor there. More like everywhere."

Job got quiet for a time and then continued. "I know it may not make much sense to you. In a way, it doesn't make sense to me either, at least not in a way that I can express it."

"Try," Eliphaz encouraged.

Job rubbed his forehead. "I was full of despair, railing against the injustice of it all, calling God to account for my condition. I wanted to die but couldn't let go. I called out for a hearing that I didn't expect to receive. And then it happened. God was here and I was there—all...all at the same time. Then God spoke."

Eliphaz could see Job's face change, that he was struggling to find the words to express what he had experienced.

"I felt God's eye on me," Job continued, "as though all of nature and beyond *breathed* the question of who was I in comparison to God? Who was the creation to question the Creator?"

Eliphaz's eyes grew wide. "What did you do?"

Job uttered a deep sigh. "I fell on my face in terror. When God had finished, there was a silence that was also a question. God was waiting for my response to what He had revealed to me. I was shaking. I don't know how I did it, but somehow I rose up and said—or thought...I'm not sure which—how small I was, like a fleck of sand, and how wondrous God was. How the fierceness of His wrath and the ocean of His mercy lit the universe with possibilities I couldn't comprehend or even imagine. How the wildness and unending revelation of His nature were beyond loss and gain, good and bad —even death and life. In the deepest part of me, I have been breathless ever since God breathed me." Job reached out to Eliphaz for the goatskin. "I need some water."

Handing the goatskin to Job, Eliphaz had one last question for him. "How has it changed you?"

After taking a long drink, Job turned to his friend. "While I am grateful for being restored in this life and while I can still feel joy and sorrow, I have seen another place. I have seen creation's possibilities and felt God's breath on my face."

Eliphaz saw the hint of a smile on Job's face that he had never seen before.

"So I am content. I am content with what is and what is to come."

COMMENTS

The Book of Job

Everyone knew that Job was a good, God-fearing man better than most. When it came to integrity and decency, he was at the top of the list. Job had been through a lot, more than most people could stand. There are people like that today that have suffered cancer, lost jobs, divorce—and every other calamity that can be imagined. "Why me, God?" is a question many of us have asked.

Job persevered throughout his travails, never giving up on God. Neither did God give up on him. At the end of Job's ordeal, we are told that God allowed Job to prosper even more than before in the ways that truly mattered. Job called God to answer for the suffering that had come to him, suffering that he felt was unjust. When Job called, God answered in a manner that changed Job's attitude and life in a profound way. Job even intervened with God on behalf of his unfaithful friends, including Eliphaz.

A case could be made that there is no more definitive treatment of suffering in the Bible than the story of Job. While perhaps not to the extent that Job suffered, we all do experience loss in our lives. Broken friendships and marriages, lost jobs, and illness come to each of us in time. What do we do when the pain comes? Where do we run to?

When everything is running smoothly or we experience unexpected benefits, we typically feel everything is as it should be. Yet, when our best-laid plans fall apart, when everything goes wrong, we ask God "why" and call on Him for a quick fix. When that doesn't happen, we get frustrated, even angry. We start with pleas and promises. If that doesn't work, we may resort to threats and denunciations. When we finally run out of excuses and demands, we end up back where we started—depending on God's mercy.

The truth is, at times each of us will experience "dark nights of the soul." During these difficult periods, how can we remain faithful? How can we hang in there and come out the other side? Will our hearts become hard as a result of such experiences or will they become more open? Sheldon Kopp, a psychotherapist, once wrote that "a heart sometimes has to be broken before it is open." Job was a broken man who, with his last stubborn ounce of faith, remained open to God's presence. He turned toward God in his darkest hour, not away from Him, and it turned his dark night into a new dawn. Will we be able to do the same when our suffering time comes?

QUESTIONS

1. Can you recall times of great physical and emotional suffering? How did you feel at your lowest point? What got you through your ordeal?

2. What do you need from your friends when your life is at a low point? What kind of friend do you need to be to someone who has cancer or some other physical or emotional illness?

3. What do you expect from God when you experience loss and sorrow? What does God expect from you during such times?

4. What lessons does the story of Job offer us in coping and growing through our dark days?

NOTES:

_____

_____

_____

_____

_____

_____

_____

_____

_____

_____

_____

Interview with Joab

8

ARE YOU THE ONE?

THE STONE CELL in the Macherus fortress was dark and damp and covered with filthy straw. The little light that filtered in came through a small, barred window a prisoner would have to strain to reach. The only inhabitant was a man sprawled in the corner with a wild, unkempt beard, covered by a rough animal skin.

Two young women approached the bars of the cell door, whispering and giggling like school children and holding their noses to ward off the stench. The older one spoke. "John the Baptizer, I am Salome, daughter of Herodias. Tonight, on my step-father, the Herod's, birthday, I danced for your head."

The man in the corner opened his eyes. Even in the dim-lit cell, the fierceness of his gaze caused the two girls to reflexively take a step backward.

Salome recovered quickly and rattled the strands of gold and silver beads draped loosely around her neck, as though she was trying to agitate a caged animal.

"Would you like to see what aroused and excited my step-father so? Should I dance for you, John the Baptizer—before the executioner arrives?"

Salome began to undulate her hips and snap her fingers as her attendant shook a small tambourine.

John said nothing. Closing his eyes, he rested his head against the cool stone wall of his cell and imagined the early morning breeze of the hills he had roamed.

Salome abruptly stopped her gyrations. Placing her hands on her hips, she shot John a petulant gaze. "I am a daughter of Herod. Show me respect or I will—"

"Or you'll do what?" John replied, not bothering to open his eyes. "Have my head? What you are is the daughter of a whore." John opened his eyes and looked at Salome, who was rendered speechless by his reprimand. "You sound like a girl but look like you come from a brothel. You smell like an animal in heat, with your painted eyes and noisy ornaments."

As the two girls gasped at John's audacity, a woman clothed in royal garments deftly stepped from the shadows of the arched doorway.

"That's enough, Salome. You and Mirsheba run along to the baths."

"But Mother-"

"I said go!" the older woman replied emphatically, pointing toward the exit.

After Salome and her attendant had made their leave, Herodias turned to John.

"Why are you so stubborn and hard-headed, John the Baptizer? It could have turned out better for you if you had only stayed in the wild and left us alone."

Brushing straw off his arm, John stared indifferently at the mother of Salome.

"I am not my daughter," Herodias scoffed. "It takes more than a hard look to intimidate me. I have survived and flourished in the world of men through much worse actions. You are a pathetic creature of the wild. Stare all you will."

John shrugged. "Woman, the hardest look you will ever see is the one looking back at you from a mirror." John folded his arms across his chest. "My poverty is a simple one—a choice I have made to live an uncluttered life. Preaching and baptizing from my perch in the hills, there are few things to distract me. I have a clear eye and a strong purpose. You, Herodias, have neither."

"Your poverty is much greater than mine. You fancy yourself a queen of sorts. Your deceit and manipulation, though clever, are shallow. You are willing to do anything—commit adultery with Herod Antipas, encourage your own flesh and blood to seduce him—anything to realize your ambitious desires. Where is Herod's hand in this? You lead him like a child to his and your ruin."

Herodias's eyes blazed as she pointed a long, painted fingernail at John. "John the Baptizer, you know nothing of my ambition or anything else about me!"

"Of course I do," John responded. "You lust for power that is driven by greed and insecurity. What you worship is fear."

"Fear?" Herodias's face flushed with anger. "I have nothing to fear, especially from the likes of you. It is you who should be afraid, for your head will be mine tomorrow."

"Perhaps," John replied. "Yet, I have only said what others in the streets and in your court are thinking. Whether I am dead or alive, their whispers and glances will feed the fear that you pretend is anger."

"Enough!" screamed Herodias. Taking a deep breath, she turned from John momentarily to regain some measure of composure. After collecting herself, Herodias pressed her face against the cell bars and smiled.

"John the Baptizer, you are a has-been. There is another now. Jesus of Nazareth is the 'latest and greatest.' Maybe he should be called 'Jesus the Baptizer,' for he will baptize many more than you. You know I speak the truth. And I dare say he will be much more reasonable to deal with than you have been. Even your own disciples are abandoning you and joining him."

John stretched his legs out on the damp straw.

"Woman, you offer me the serpent's smile. What happens to me is of little importance compared to the One who comes after me."

Herodias hissed a whisper in response. "Poor John the Baptizer. Nothing but a has-been. Before I have thrown your head to the dogs and they have licked your skull clean, you will be no more than a distant memory."

Herodias left as quickly as she appeared, with a rustle of her robes and a scornful laugh.

John looked up at the small window in his cell. Night would be coming soon. He had to admit to himself that he was bone-tired as the grief of doubt washed over him. He hoped his trusted disciple and friend, Simon Jonas, had taken his message to Jesus.

John drank some of the brackish water that was offered to him by a sympathetic guard, but had no appetite for the piece of stale bread. As many condemned men do the night before their execution, he slept in fits and fragments.

John awoke just before dawn to the sound of his name.

"Simon Jonas, is that you?"

"No, my friend."

John moved to the small cell window, straining to see through the first rays of dawn's light.

"Who is it, then?" he cried, grasping the window's bars with both hands.

"It is me."

"Jesus?"

"Yes, John. I have come to you."

"Am I dreaming? Is this only a condemned man's dream?"

"No, John. You are not dreaming. How are you?"

"Well enough, considering...."

"Do you remember when we were children playing together—our mothers watching us and laughing?"

John's face softened at the thought of it.

"Do you remember the day you baptized me in the River Jordan?"

John nodded his head.

"John, I have come to answer your question." John's voice cracked as he felt Jesus' hand cover his. "Are you...are you the One?"

"Who do you say I am?" Jesus replied. "What does your heart tell you?"

"I believe, but am afraid."

"Yes," Jesus responded softly. "You are afraid, but I tell you the truth. My love for you is stronger than your fear."

John gripped Jesus' hands. "I tried to prepare the way for you."

"I know you did, my friend. You were the bridge from the old way to the new. I couldn't have done it without you."

John sighed. "Today...in a little while...."

Jesus squeezed John's hand. "Today, I will be with you. And remember, John."

"Remember what?"

"Today is not the end, but the beginning."

The clatter of the approaching guards signaled that the time had come. As they prepared him for the executioner, Herodias appeared. Her eyes danced behind her veil with the fever of vengeance. Thrusting a silver platter toward him, she could barely restrain her excitement.

"John the Baptizer, a new day is upon us. Your head will make a fine centerpiece for my platter."

John looked at Herodias with a calmness she found strangely unsettling.

"Woman, you can have my head, but not my heart. You can take my life, but not my faith."

John knelt before the executioner and closed his eyes.

A spring rain brought forth new life and a burst of color. The River Jordan had never looked more beautiful. John knelt down to drink from it.

COMMENTS

Matthew 11:2-15

Awaiting execution, John sent his disciples to ask Jesus if He was the One. While we do not know his reasons, we do know that doubt often creeps into the best of us when we face difficult situations. Perhaps it was the same for John.

John had prepared the way for one who was greater than he. He had remained faithful to his task like other prophets before him, calling Herod and Herodias to account for their misdeeds and unfaithfulness. With the help of her seductive daughter, Salome, Herodias finally found a way to silence John. All of his hard work had brought him to the executioner's sword.

Frederick Buechner once wrote, "Doubt is the ants in the pants of faith." We all want proof in matters of faith, but then, if something could be proven, faith wouldn't be required. Blind faith doesn't require personal struggle and doubt like that experienced by John. For example, fanatics who follow tyrants are not inclined to question their leader's actions or motives. They simply do what they are told, no matter what amount of suffering to themselves or innocent victims is the result. The kind of dynamic faith John had was another matter. His faith was the result of his mind interacting with his heart, and included reflection, prayer, and action. When faced with his impending death at the hands of Herod and Herodias, he sought reassurance that his faith and commitment to "One greater than I" wasn't in vain.

Believing seems much easier when no sacrifice is required. Faith and belief may also be used by some today, as it was thousands of years ago, as a kind of superstitious talisman to ward off sickness or ensure wealth and prosperity. Yet, like John, our faith is tested when we or our loved ones are experiencing the final stages of cancer, a bankrupt career, or a failed marriage. Death comes to us in many forms, degrees, and faces.

What we can learn from this story, among other things, is that our faith and beliefs will inevitably be tested—sometimes in dramatic and sacrificial ways—and not always have happy endings as far as this life is concerned. We can denounce or run away from our faith because it didn't produce the outcome we desired or, like John, we can persevere and embrace its promise in our darkest of times. Through our faith we can leap into the unknown, into the arms of the love in which we placed our trust. And like Jesus said to

John in the story, we can rest assured that when our time comes, "it is not the end, but the beginning."

QUESTIONS

1. Some might question John's faith, given his previous baptism of Jesus and his declaration about Jesus' purpose and mission. Why would he have even the smallest doubt after such an event?

2. Can you think of times when your faith was shattered along with your dreams? What stages did you go through as you tried to make sense of your life?

3. Countless people of faith throughout history have chosen death rather than renounce their beliefs. Try to put yourself in their place. Are you certain you would accept shame, humiliation, torture, and execution rather than renounce your faith? Jesus did, but would we?

4. Like John the Baptist, we all need reassurance when our faith is severely tested. Does Christ offer us reassurance during such times? In what forms might it come?

NOTES:

_____

_____

_____

_____

_____

_____

_____

_____

_____

Interview with Joab

_____

_____

_____

_____

_____

_____

9

LONG, HARD ROAD

THE EMACIATED YOUNG man hunched down among the swine, grabbing and gobbling up anything he could find among the slop that was edible. The hogs squealed and grunted their displeasure toward the unwelcome intruder interrupting their feeding time.

A rotten piece of fruit splattered against the young man's head. Men laughed outside the holding pen. "Good shot, Hezra," crowed one of the more rowdy companions, "and with a bellyful of wine, at that!"

Hezra grasped the fence with both hands and glowered at the young man who had stopped eating and dropped his head in shame.

"Jesse Bar-Joseph, it is good to see that you are eating well."

The group of men again roared with laughter.

"What do you say now, great Jesse? You, who would not give me the time of day when you first came to our land, riding on a fine mule and loaded with your father's riches. Where are your man-servants and your mule? Where are you riches? What say you, Jesse Bar-Joseph?"

The young man said nothing in reply, staring at the mud covering his bare feet.

Tossing another piece of over-ripe fruit at the hapless young man and then another, Hezra continued. "You are wise not to answer. You, who held yourself in such high esteem, have fallen so low that you have hired yourself out to me, a man who at one time you thought beneath you."

Hezra wiped his hands on a towel one of his servants offered him before turning back to the forlorn young man. This time the tone in his voice was dead serious.

"Jesse Bar-Joseph, you are worth less to me than one of these swine. If I hear of you eating food that was prepared for them again, you will be punished." With that final comment, Hezra turned abruptly and walked away, his companions and servants following.

Jesse stood in the muck and the cold of the night and cried. He covered his face with his hands, his body wracked with the sobs of one who had lost all hope.

"Come, Jesse, you need to rest. Morning will come soon."

Jesse rubbed his eyes. "Abatha, what is to come of me?"

The old man took Jesse by the arm and led him toward the barn where the slaves and servants slept. "Come, we will talk in the morning. Everything will be clearer in the morning."

The sun was hot. Two men, one young and the other old, worked side by side in the field. It would be at least an hour until their next water break. Jesse's and Abatha's hoes worked in a kind of rhythmic duet, chopping the soil and removing weeds that could choke the tender shoots trying to mature into the fall's wheat.

Jesse wiped the sweat streaming from his brow. "Abatha, how do you do it?"

"Do what, my young friend?"

"Work the way you do at the age you are? You eat very little, yet never seem to tire—even when we have to walk to distant fields. And your legs—they are scarred and you walk with a limp. I don't see how you walk at all."

The corners of Abatha's mouth turned into the most subtle of smiles. "Jesse, Jesse. You see so much. You see so little."

Jesse turned and looked at his companion. "I don't understand."

Abatha sighed. "What you have been doing for a short while, I have been doing for a long time. You seem to forget that I am a slave while you are not. You can choose to leave when you have worked off your debt. And of course, I cannot."

"It all seems so unfair and hopeless," Jesse retorted.

"What is hope, young Jesse?" Abatha chuckled softly. "You hope for less toil and hardship for which you expend great energy and effort. I also work, but do not toil. I am not attached to my effort or its outcome. You hope for more food—for a full belly. My heart is full. It satisfies a deeper hunger."

Jesse interrupted his older friend. "That's all well and good, but you want your freedom from this hell-hole as much as I do. I have heard from others that you once tried to escape and return to your home land in North Africa. When they caught you, they broke both your legs."

The two men worked for a while in silence. The only sound was that of the overseer's shouts of admonishment and the occasional crack of his whip.

Finally, the water boy arrived. Abatha drank his fill and passed the water skin to Jesse. The two friends sat on the ground and rested while the water boy made his rounds to the other men working in their group.

Long, Hard Road

Abatha turned to Jesse and looked deep into his eyes. "It is true as you say. Many years ago, I felt as you do and tried to escape. They caught me, beat me, and broke both my legs. I wanted to die. But slowly—little by little —a great change took place in me. The freedom you hope for upon release from your debt, I have already found in, as you refer to it, this hell-hole."

"But how?" Jesse replied. "How could you be content in this place?"

Abatha smiled once more at his young friend and pointed to his own heart. "Because this is the place where I live—maybe the only place where life is really possible."

Abatha could see the confusion in Jesse's eyes.

"Dear Jesse, can't you see that our bodies are fading—that we are returning to dust? That is why I am an old man and you are a young man. But while you may be much younger than me, we are still—both you and I—in the same line. I'm just further along than you. Like it or not, you will follow in my footsteps."

Abatha reached out and took Jesse's hand and placed it on the young man's heart.

"Remember, until you are free here, you will be a slave to whatever you fear, lust for, and envy out in the world."

The overseer shouted and the water boy scurried along to the next field as the men in Abatha and Jesse's group returned to their labor. They worked in silence for the rest of the day as Jesse thought about his friend's words.

———

Jesse and Abatha leaned against the barnyard fence near the remains of the cook-fire and looked up at a star-lit night sky. Abatha chewed on a twig while Jesse looked at the old man with a mix of wonder, curiosity, and respect.

"Abatha, my time will be up in seven days. What am I to do? Where am I to go?"

Abatha continued chewing on the twig. "Indeed, young Jesse. Indeed."

"I have nothing. I squandered the inheritance my father gave me. Showed him and my brother no respect. Left them in a huff and my mother in tears. I made it clear that the last thing they would see of me was the backside of my mule." Jesse kicked a clump of sand. "I have nothing. I am nothing."

Abatha took the twig from his mouth and turned his face toward Jesse. "Are you not still your father's son?"

Jesse rubbed his arm. "Maybe, but I'm not worthy to be called his son. He's probably disowned me. It's what I deserve. I've dishonored them all."

"Ah, what one deserves." Abatha rubbed his chin. "Always a challenging question."

Jesse looked squarely at Abatha. "The truth is I have been thinking lately about returning home, begging for my father's forgiveness, and asking not to be restored to my former place but just to be one of his workers. My father is nothing like Hezra. All his workers are treated fairly. Even the lowliest worker has a full belly and a warm fire at night."

Jesse warmed his hands over the dying embers of the evening's cookfire.

"I had a strange dream last night about my father. I dreamed my father was waiting for me to come home, down by the gate to the main road. He was waiting in the dark. I know—it was just a dream…but it got me to thinking."

Abatha placed his right hand on Jesse's shoulder. "Was it a dream? Or was it the hope of a father's love reaching across these many miles through the dark to you, his son?" Abatha squeezed his young friend's shoulder. "You may have been out of your father's sight, but not out of his heart."

As he lay down on his sleeping mat, the thought of Abatha's words made Jesse smile like he used to when he was a boy. As he drifted off to sleep, Jesse could feel the distant echo of his father's voice carried by a nighttime breeze whispering his name.

COMMENTS

Luke 15:11-32

As children, we have all been prodigal sons and daughters in one way or another, and as parents, we have struggled with our own children's decisions to rebel and go their own way. In Luke, we see a prodigal son that was immature, self-important, and impulsive. He took his inheritance, broke his father's heart, and left his elder brother to do all the work while he lived it up among the bright lights in the big city.

Like many of our own selfish and impulsive choices, the outcomes the prodigal son experienced made him yearn to rebuild the bridges he had burned. Like us in similar situations, the hole he found himself in was deep and dark.

We live in a world where children often seem to be calling the shots in families, demanding this toy or that video game or the latest and greatest fashion accessory. We hustle them from one activity to another, right into their teenage years. As our teenagers merge into young adulthood, their demands may carry ever-increasing price tags. Cars, college, clothes, and an eventful social life are expected by many of our sons and daughters, no matter what the costs. Where do we draw the line? If we refuse, a request may become a demand and perhaps even a threat of cutting off contact.

Two of the themes examined in this story are the consequences of indulgence and arrogance, and learning the lesson of humility. A prodigal son has demanded from his father and received his inheritance, which he has squandered away in short order. He has gone from being a rebellious, even arrogant, big-spender to an indentured servant for someone he had formerly looked down upon. Hungry and humiliated, he would have lost all hope were it not for the wise old slave who befriended him. The prodigal son, like many of us, learned the lesson of humility the hard way. His old friend turns him away from despair toward the possibility of grace in returning home.

No matter what we have done—what poor choices we have made, we can find our way back to forgiveness and fellowship. Yet, part of the price of our ticket back home is that, like the prodigal son, we must first eat the "husks" we have created through our choices. Where life's mistakes are concerned, it is an "all you can eat buffet."

QUESTIONS

1. What are some of the reasons the "prodigal" son may have become selfish and self-indulgent? His older brother remained faithful. Why didn't he?

2. Like the prodigal son, does each of us get a "taste of our own medicine" at one time or another in our lives?

3. Do we all need a friend like Abatha to encourage us and help us get back on track with our lives when we have reached the end of a destructive path? Can you think of any Abathas that helped you in some of your darkest moments? Did you let them know how much they meant to you?

4. Perhaps Jesse's father both loved and spoiled him. Although the consequences of Jesse's choices and his father's indulgence are apparent, what role may his father's love have played in his choosing to return home?

5. In one way or another, at one time or another, are we all prodigal sons and daughters? How can we move from the place or relationship we find ourselves in and return to where we need to be?

Notes:

_____

_____

_____

_____

_____

_____

_____

_____

Long, Hard Road

_____

_____

_____

_____

_____

_____

_____

_____

10

THE FIRST STONE

THE AROMA OF steaming lentils, onions, and garlic wafted from the cook-pot. A young woman grasped a wooden ladle with both hands and stirred the pot's contents with an even and energetic stroke. An older woman entered the small house of stone and wood, carrying a large clay pitcher of fresh water on her shoulder. She touched a stone on a small shelf next to the door and smiled at the sight of the young woman stirring the stew with such determined deliberation.

"Daughter, you stir with such conviction."

"I am determined to get it right this time. There will be nothing sticking to the bottom of this pot if I have anything to do about it," the young woman replied, wiping the sweat from her brow.

The older woman laughed as she poured a small amount of water into the cook-pot before placing the pitcher in the window so the evening breeze could keep it cool.

"Did you remember to add the extra seasoning like I told you?"

"Yes, mother. Here, taste it."

The older woman accepted the ladle from her daughter. Tasting the stew, she smacked her lips for emphasis. "Very good, Hester, very tasty indeed."

Standing up and placing her hands on her hips, Hester stared at the object of her labor. "Maybe Artemas will bring us a piece of fish for the stew since he and Uncle Hanan went to Galilee on business."

"Perhaps," her mother replied. "Either way, the stew will be good because we will be eating it together."

A few hours later, Artemas sopped up the last of the stew with a piece of bread and popped it into his mouth.

"You are becoming a better cook, little sister. Tonight my belly is full and I don't feel the least bit sick."

Hester threw the wooden spoon at her brother, who ducked. "You deserve to be sick for not bringing us a piece of fish home for our supper!"

Artemas wiped his hands on his tunic. "You know I would if I could, but times are hard. All Uncle Hanan had for us to eat were a handful of olives and a loaf of barley. The flock hasn't grown as much as he and I had hoped.

Between the thieves and the wolves, we have lost more than we gained with last spring's births. He even let a more experienced shepherd go just to keep me on."

The older woman rose from her mat and looked at her son and daughter. "We have much to be grateful for. For many years your Uncle Hanan has been more than good to us. Since the two of you were small children, he has provided for us time and again through thick and thin."

Artemas stretched out on his mat. "I will have to return to the fields before night falls to relieve one of the shepherds. His wife is expected to deliver their first child."

"I remembered, son. I have packed some dried figs and raisins along with a piece of bread and cheese for you. You will also find a horn packed with olive oil and your flask full of fresh water. You rest while your sister and I clean up. I will wake you when it's time to leave."

Artemas had left for the flocks with hugs from his mother and sister. The two women had accompanied him to the edge of the village and were making their way back home. People were still scattered about, some carrying full pitchers from the well while others stood or sat together in small groups catching up on the day's news and gossip. Smells of evening meals just finished or begun mingled with the haunting sound of a flute. Darkness would fall within the hour.

Hester preceded her mother into the small, single-room dwelling place they called home. Her mother followed, touching the stone on the shelf as she entered.

Refilling the oil lamp, Hester sat down next to her mother. "Why do you always touch that stone by the door every time you leave or enter our home?"

"My girl of many questions," her mother replied, smiling. "Like I have told you so many times before, dear Hester, I will answer your questions when the time is right. When—"

"I know, I know," Hester interrupted. "But the right time never seems to come."

"You are still a young girl."

"I am fourteen years old, Mother. Old enough to get married. Two from our village are betrothed who are younger than me."

Hester lay down on her mat and turned on her side away from her mother, who looked at her daughter but said nothing as the sounds of the evening moved toward the stillness of nightfall.

The older woman lit the oil lamp and stared in silence at the flicker of its flame for a long time before reaching to awaken her daughter again.

Hester sat up, rubbing the sleep from her eyes. "What is it, Mother? Is it time to get up?"

"No, it is time to answer your questions. Where would you like to start?"

Hester watched as her mother poured herself a cup of water, surprised. She started with the question that was most important to her.

"Why did Father leave us?"

Her mother's hand shook as she sipped from the cup.

"Because I was unfaithful to him."

"Unfaithful?"

Her mother put the cup down and looked at her puzzled daughter.

"Yes, unfaithful. We lived in Jerusalem at the time. You were barely a toddler, your brother two years older. Your father was a spice merchant and gone much of the time. I was lonely and I made a terrible mistake."

Hester was stunned. "You have always been a good mother."

"A better mother than wife," her mother replied with a sad smile.

The two sat in silence until her mother resumed her confession.

"Our next door neighbor was a widower who was a wine merchant. He began to show an interest in me."

"Didn't people notice what was going on? Didn't they talk?" Hester interjected.

"Yes, on both accounts. Your Uncle Hanan warned me."

"Why didn't you listen to him?"

Hester's mother stared at her empty cup. "That is a good question, daughter, and one that I have asked myself countless times. I was young and foolish. Too much loneliness. Too much attention. Too much wine. Take your pick."

Hester reached out and took her mother's hand in hers. "You could have been brought before the elders and stoned to death had they found out what you were doing."

"They did find out."

Hester brought her hand to her mouth in shock. "They found out?"

"Yes."

Hester's mother took another sip of water. "The elders along with some scribes and Pharisees dragged me before the rabbi, Jesus, and asked him to render a proper judgment."

"Jesus of Nazareth?"

"Yes, daughter, Jesus of Nazareth."

"Were you scared?"

Hester's mother smiled wearily. "I was very frightened…even more ashamed."

"What did he say?"

"First, he knelt down and wrote something on the ground with his finger. Then he rose and faced the men who had brought me before him and spoke to them."

"What did he say to them?" Hester asked in wide-eyed amazement.

"He said, 'Let him who is without sin among you be the first to throw a stone at her,'" Hester's mother replied in a cracked voice.

"He said that?"

"Yes, my daughter, that is what he said."

"What did the men do?"

"They left."

"Then what?"

"Then the Master turned to me and said, 'Where are they? Has no one condemned you?' And I answered him, 'No one, Lord.'" Hester's mother's face was flushed and her eyes bright with remembering. "The Master said, 'Neither do I condemn you. Go now and leave your life of sin.' Before I turned to leave, he bent down and picked up a stone and handed it to me."

"And then?"

"And then I left and returned home."

Hester was silent, pondering what she had heard. "Is that when Father left?"

"Yes. I deserved no less. I brought shame and dishonor to him and both of our families. He divorced me and we moved here."

"But Uncle Hanan?"

Hester's mother wiped her eyes. "Your father's brother was the only one in the family who didn't disown me. Like the Master, he showed me mercy when justice was called for."

Hester reached out and embraced her mother. The two held each other in silence.

Stroking her daughter's hair, Hester's mother looked deep into her daughter's eyes. "We are here—you, Artemas, and me—because of the mercy of the Master and the kindness of your Uncle Hanan. It is time for us to sleep now."

Mother and daughter lay side by side in the darkness, each left to her own thoughts.

"Mother."

"Yes?"

"I have one more question."

"What is it?"

"Why did Jesus give you that stone, and why do you touch it each time you leave and enter our home?"

"I can't say for sure, but the stone, the first one of many that was to be an instrument of my death, was given to me as a gift. The Master gave me back my life. He loved me enough to give me a second chance. I touch that gift many times each day as a reminder of all the tender mercies I have experienced since meeting him those many years ago."

COMMENTS

John 8:1-11

A woman caught in the act of adultery was brought before Jesus. The penalty was clear and simple: death by stoning. The group of men who brought her before Jesus awaited his answer to the verdict.

After Jesus wrote something on the ground, He addressed the group of men. His moral message was just as clear and simple as was their legal verdict. No one chose to cast the first stone. Like us, all were guilty as charged. Each man left, starting with the oldest.

Unhappy marriages, predatory Romeos and Juliets, and even domestic abuse are just some of the reasons husbands and wives violate their marriage vows. We don't really know why the woman committed adultery in the case brought before Jesus, and we can imagine that the men who brought her probably had a variety of motives for dragging her into His presence. What we do know is that His response turned the legal justice of the day on its ear. He suggested the opposite of what the Law called for.

While most of us may not betray our marriage, we have all been both victims and offenders regarding "crimes of the heart." When we get hurt— when our trust has been betrayed and our hearts broken—we are inclined to want justice and retribution. Of course, when we are the betrayer, when our off-handed comment has harmed a friend, we yearn for forgiveness and for the relationship we have broken to be restored.

In the end, we can't have it both ways. Are we on the side of mercy or retribution? The Law demanded justice, yet Jesus—a higher standard— chose to be merciful. Can we do no less?

We don't know what happened to the woman in the story, but whatever happened, it was a day she would never forget—the day she won the mercy lottery.

QUESTIONS

1. There are different interpretations regarding the legal and moral ramifications concerning the story about Jesus and the adulteress. Whatever the reasons the Pharisees and Sadducees had for bringing the accused woman before Jesus, we can safely assume as on previous occasions, they wanted to put Him on the spot. What do you think may be some of the reasons they brought her before Jesus? Why not a thief or a cheat? Why a woman caught in adultery?

2. What lesson was Jesus trying to teach the elders in suggesting who among them might throw the first stone? Why do you think the oldest among the group of accusers were the first to leave after Jesus' pronouncement?

3. What do you think Jesus may have said to the husband of the adulteress if He had encountered him?

4. Why do you and I often find it so easy to hold a grudge and so difficult to forgive one who we feel has betrayed our trust and taken advantage of us?

NOTES:

_____

_____

_____

_____

_____

_____

_____

_____

The First Stone

_____

_____

_____

_____

_____

_____

_____

_____

11

KEEPER OF THE COIN

A SMALL FIRE POPPED and crackled against the chill of the night, throwing flickering shadows across a rock ledge where a man huddled into its warmth, rubbing his hands together and muttering to himself.

"Never seen a night so cold this time of the year. Nor a heart so cold. Cold. Cold. Cold." Simon Peter stared deeply into the dancing flames, dumbstruck by recent events. "Why did I do it?" he cried. "Why?"

Peter poked at the fire with a stick, sending sparks spiraling up into the night sky. He was numb with confusion and remorse, not knowing what to think or feel. His forlorn laugh of self-derision melded with the sound of the fire.

"Simon Peter, you are no rock—no man of action. You are a cold-hearted coward full of fear and weakness. You are worse than nothing."

He added more wood to the fire as the flames leaped up into the night sky.

"I'm all cried out. Fire, no matter how hot I make you, you can't chase the chill from my soul."

Peter was startled by a voice from the darkness.

"Friend, may I warm myself by your fire before continuing on my way?"

Peter's right hand reached for the leather scabbard which held his sword. He studied the lone man standing at the edge of the fire's light before responding. Was the stranger a simple journeyman in need of a fire's warmth or was he the bait for his fellow bandits hiding nearby? Peter didn't know which one he was, but after the last several days, he didn't much care.

He shrugged. "Come. Share my fire. There's wine in the skin to my left and a bit of bread as well. You are welcome to both."

The stranger stepped from the shadows toward the fire, the hood of his cloak concealing most of his features. Sitting down cross-legged, he accepted the wineskin from Peter.

"It's late to be walking these roads with all the bandits and such about."

Waving off Peter's offer of bread, the stranger drank from the wineskin and handed it back to him. The two men sat and watched the fire. In spite of himself, Peter was glad for the company.

"Where you from?"

"Here and there," the stranger replied, then fell silent.

After a few moments, Peter queried the stranger once more.

"Where you headed?"

The stranger rubbed his hands together over the flames.

"Just down the road. Not far from here."

Peter looked up from the fire.

"Just down the road? The next town is a full day's walk from here."

The stranger shrugged but didn't reply.

The uneasiness Peter felt when the stranger first appeared out of nowhere returned. His eyes searched the perimeter of his camp, looking for signs of outlaws.

"I'm alone," the stranger said. "You are in no danger from me."

Peter rested his hand on the hilt of his scabbard just the same. "What you say doesn't add up. Where do you come from?"

"Jerusalem."

Peter looked more closely at the stranger. "There's something about you. You remind me of somebody I once knew." He could feel his blood rising. "What were you doing in Jerusalem?"

Rising to his feet, the stranger pulled back his hooded cloak and replied, "I was betraying our Master."

"Judas Iscariot!" Peter exclaimed as he leapt to his feet, drawing his sword.

"Yes, that would be me."

"You...you..." Peter sputtered, glaring at his former companion.

Grief dropped across Judas' face as he interrupted Peter. "Yes, Peter. I am the great betrayer." Pulling apart the upper portion of his tunic with both hands, Judas bared his chest.

"Why don't you put your sword to good use? If you can cut off the high priest's servant's ear, finding my heart with the point of your sword should be easy. Go ahead. Do us both a favor."

Suddenly Peter's shoulders sagged as his gaze returned to the fire. "If I use my sword on anyone, it should be myself. You aren't the only one who betrayed our Master. I denied Him three times, just like He said I would. The last time, I cursed like a sailor, I was so scared. The worst of it was when I felt His gaze after that third time as the guards led Him away. I'll never forget that look."

Judas looked at Peter. "Your betrayal was born of fear—a spontaneous reaction without thought or genuine malice. Besides, after Jesus predicted your denial, He said He would pray for you, did He not?"

Peter nodded his head.

Judas adjusted his tunic and pulled his cloak back around his shoulders. "My betrayal was calculated. Yours wasn't. I allowed myself to be seduced by Deseas, Caiaphas's assistant. You were trying to protect yourself. While what you did may have been cowardly, it didn't put our Rabbi in harm's way. My choice did."

Judas tightened the rope belt around his waist.

"I should be on my way. Like I told you earlier, I have an appointment to keep."

Peter reached for the wineskin and took a sip. He sat down by the fire and motioned for Judas to do the same.

"Why, Judas? Why did you do it?"

Judas sat across from Peter and drank deeply from the wineskin when Peter offered it to him again. He looked into the burning embers for a long time before responding to Peter's question.

"I'm not sure I can give you a clear answer. In a way, there are several reasons. But then again, there are none."

Judas drank once more from the wineskin.

"As you know, things were chaotic at the end. I am a person of logic, and in one sense—maybe it was only wishful thinking—it seemed logical to me that the kingdom was, indeed, at hand. Our entry into Jerusalem. The cheering crowds. Everything seemed to be falling in place. Except I couldn't get Jesus to stay focused and take advantage of our opportunity. He seemed more and more preoccupied—even distant at times. I became increasingly disappointed, even despondent that our—that Jesus'—big chance was slipping away. So I guess disappointment was one reason."

Judas took another sip and handed the wineskin back to Peter.

"Then as the crowds began to drift away, I became concerned about our and Jesus' safety. I knew Caiaphas and his henchmen would move against us if our popularity with the people faded."

Peter threw another piece of wood on the fire. "Is that when Deseas came forward? I remember seeing him when the Master chased the money-changers out of the temple."

"Actually, I knew Deseas before we came to Jerusalem. He was with the other Pharisees who came to hear Jesus teach. Unlike some of the others, he seemed impressed with the Master, especially the sermon on the mount. But you are right in a sense. It wasn't until after the incident at the temple that Deseas told me of his influence with the high priest. He seemed genuinely concerned about our safety. I should have known better, but I was afraid of what the future held. Deseas assured me that if I pointed out Jesus, He would be chastised, but after that He would be released—that all the high priest was really interested in was keeping everything calm during Passover with minimum disruptions."

Peter shook his head in dismay.

"I know, Peter. I know. I was on a fool's errand, and am now a damned fool because of it."

The silence returned as the two disciples watched the fire.

"No one is beyond the reach and mercy of our Master," Peter replied. "He has proven it time and time again."

Judas smiled wearily. "I am afraid I am. You are to be the 'rock.' I have been but the keeper of the coin, which, as you have probably heard, was also part of the transaction of betrayal. Thirty pieces of silver to be exact."

Peter began to rock back and forth. "I heard that you didn't take the money."

Judas picked up a rock and tossed it into the fire. "I took it. Nothing like gold or silver to catch the eye of a keeper of the coin. When I realized what Deseas and Caiaphas were up to, I didn't want it. They wouldn't take it back, so I threw the coins at them and left." Judas looked up from the fire at Peter. "Caiaphas has seen to the death of Jesus, scattered our brothers, and kept his blood money. For him, a win-win situation. But then, he couldn't have done it without me."

"Still, Judas, the Master is not like us. Even when He was upset, He did not hold onto to His anger. It was He who said we must 'forgive seventy times seven.' I cannot believe He would do less than He has instructed us to do. He said He would come back in three days, and tomorrow is—"

"It's a nice thought, and I wish I could believe you," Judas interrupted. "The truth is, I don't deserve forgiveness. If our Rabbi remains cold in the grave, I have sent a good, innocent man to His death. If He is resurrected, justice will demand my life, or worse. Either way, it's over for me."

Peter pointed his finger at Judas. "I'm telling you straight out, Judas—if there is a chance for me, there is also a chance for you. The One who loved us enough to call us as His disciples is also the One who will, in the end, judge us."

Judas shrugged. "Another sip of wine, please?"

Peter handed him the wineskin.

After he had finished, Judas wiped his mouth with the hem of his cloak. "Like I said before, my passionate and compassionate Peter, you were His rock. I was but His accountant, the keeper of the coin, the man with the moneybag."

Peter interrupted. "But you made it all work! You made each coin count —food, lodging, and help for the poor. We all marveled at your skill. I even heard the Master comment on how resourceful you were."

Judas's face softened. "Still, I didn't have your passion and spontaneity. You celebrated Mary washing the Master's feet with expensive perfume while I complained. You recognized the gift of her sacrifice while all I saw was its monetary value. I guess I have always been a man of numbers. I felt joy when I served our Master, but I also felt even more joy when the numbers added up—when the odds seemed to clearly point to a positive outcome. In a way, I served two masters."

"I've never really had a head for numbers," Peter replied.

"True enough, Peter. You were a man of passion and conviction—a man of action. You were always willing to go for broke—like when you walked to Jesus during that storm at sea. While the others and I were hanging on to the sides of the boat for dear life and worrying about our chances of making it to the safety of shore, you threw caution to the wind and responded to the Master's call against all odds, even though it seemed impossible to the rest of us."

Peter raised his eyebrows. "But I sank. Could have drowned had it not been for the Master."

"Still," Judas replied, "you jumped. The rest of us had more faith in a leaky boat than the Master's command."

"The truth is, Peter, I have always been too much about the numbers, the money and the odds. As I said before, going into Jerusalem with the crowds shouting praises to Jesus…every thing seemed to be falling into place. The birth of a new movement that could influence the Sanhedrin—maybe even change the world!"

"We all felt that way," Peter interjected.

"Yes, but then Jesus informed us that His kingdom was not of this world and that He would be leaving," Judas continued. "I went in short order from high hopes to despair. And some resentment, too. From planning budgets for the Master's follow-up to His triumphant entry into Jerusalem…to fear."

"Yes," Peter replied. "We were all confused and disheartened. That crowing cock reminded me how afraid I was—what a fraud and hypocrite I am."

Judas held the outstretched palms of his hands over the burning embers before rising to his feet.

"It's time I move on. I have an appointment to keep. I thank you for your hospitality."

Peter rose as well. "Judas, why don't you stay with me here by the fire? The night is almost done and tomorrow will be the third day. Some, like Thomas, doubt that Jesus will return, but I believe that He will. You and I can go to Him together."

Judas placed his hands on Peter's shoulders. "Some rise. Others fall. The night calls me, the morning you. My hope is that Jesus and you, my friend, will rise. As for me, my appointment won't wait."

As Judas walked into what was left of the darkness, he turned one last time to Peter.

"I do have one last favor to ask of you."

"What is it, Judas?"

"If you do see our Master, tell him that I am sorry for what I did—that I did love Him…."

Judas' voice trailed off as he turned and walked away.

COMMENTS

Matthew 26: 21-25; 34-35; 69-75 and 27:3-5.

Judas was the money man, the original treasurer of the ministry's funds. If there had been a Wall Street in Jerusalem, that might well be where he would have come from. Yet Judas was more than that. While he had an accountant's mindset, he also—at least in the beginning—had a disciple's heart. After all, Jesus did choose him to become a part of the inner circle, one of the original twelve disciples. He started out handling the money, and at least in part, the money ended up handling him. He tried to give back the thirty pieces of silver, but unfortunately he could not take back the choice he made or the consequences that followed.

Two themes seem to stand out in the story of Peter and Judas. The primary theme addresses the act of betrayal and how one who acts in such a manner responds to his or her deed. A second, less obvious but still potent, theme has to do with money. While money is an important issue to all of us and being financially responsible is an important attribute, overreliance on money can contribute to an attitude where one comes to believe that there is no problem that enough money cannot solve. Judas may not have entirely felt that way, but his accountant's mentality concerning keeping the "books in order" played well to an attitude based upon a kind of logic where events and relationships needed to "add up." Of course, it is often easier to balance the books than one's life. In reality, life often doesn't add up. Whatever the motives and reasons, Judas—as well as Peter—betrayed Jesus.

While perhaps, in most cases, betrayal does not occur on the magnitude of Judas's actions, it is nonetheless a familiar feature of the human condition. Delilah betrayed Samson, and Benedict Arnold his fellow patriots in a fledgling democracy that was to become the United States of America. There are examples of kings, presidents, and all other sorts of noteworthy persons throughout history who have betrayed and deceived their spouses, other family members, friends, and all manner of others who have trusted them. Some betrayed for money, others for power, pleasure, or just because they could.

All of us know how it feels to be both victims and perpetrators of betrayal. Although not on the same scale, both Judas and Peter betrayed the confidence of Jesus. Both were His disciples and both were dedicated to serving Jesus' purpose and mission. It is interesting that Peter, the one who the Scriptures suggest may have been closer in terms of his affection for Jesus, seemed to have a very different reaction to his transgression than did the more objective and analytical Judas. Though it appears both disciples felt terrible about what they had done, it seems that one held out hope of forgiveness and reconciliation, while the other could not imagine or accept such a possibility—the possibility that nothing was beyond the love of their Master. One faced, even embraced, his shame and turned toward the love he trusted, while the other withdrew, fearing a judgment that unfortunately became a self-fulfilling prophecy.

QUESTIONS

1. What would your reaction have been if you had done what Peter or Judas did? Can you think of any ways you may have some of the weaknesses Peter or Judas displayed?

2. Can you remember a time when you did not speak up when others were maligning a friend or acquaintance in your presence out of fear that they might criticize or reject you?

3. Have you ever criticized or undermined someone at work, church, or in a social setting in an attempt to gain an advantage in the eyes of others?

4. Do we, on occasion, focus too much on money in solving our family's as well as our own problems? When we move from the desire to earn "enough" money to provide for our family's *needs* to a desire for financial wealth in order to satisfy all of their and our *wants*, are we in danger of losing our spiritual priority and focus? Can you think of any examples where such a focus was misapplied? What might the consequences be of such actions?

5. If Jesus had appeared around that imaginary campfire where Peter and Judas sat, what do you think He might have said to them?

NOTES:

_____

_____

_____

_____

_____

_____

_____

12

PILATE'S WIFE

THE FULL MOON swept the hillsides with a soft light. A gentle breeze moved the cool night air across the landscape. Although she was a young girl, Claudia felt safe as she walked in the moonlight. She could see the pathway clearly and, for a moment, felt serene and confident, surrounded by an illuminated, peaceful countryside.

But slowly, as before, she began to feel a sense of uneasiness tinged with dread about a dark hill that was ahead of her, that awaited her unseen in the cascading light of the full moon but somehow out there, drawing her closer with each step.

Claudia awoke with a start, her face moist and clammy.

"Miriam, where are you?"

A young woman hurried to her bedside. "The dreams come again?" She poured her a cup of fresh water.

"Yes, Miriam. They seem to be coming more frequently."

"Should I call for the physician?"

"No," Claudia replied, sitting up. "I'm always on the same path. Each time further along and a bit older. The moon is full. The night air is pleasant. And the surroundings are peaceful."

Miriam put the pitcher of water down and began to comb the hair of the governor's wife. "Where does the path lead?"

Claudia rubbed her eyes. "That's the problem. I don't know. As beautiful and peaceful as the surroundings are, I know that a dark place is up ahead. I can't see it, but I know it's there—pulling me toward it. Waiting for me to arrive."

"That sounds frightening. Can you not turn around or stop and rest?"

Claudia smiled to herself. For a slave girl, Miriam was inquisitive and even bold at times. That's what she liked about her. Not a dullard like so many of her attendants. Miriam knew she was legally a slave, but saw herself as more than that. Her loyalty was born out of respect and her affection was genuine, attributes Claudia appreciated.

"Miriam, I would like to turn around, but somehow I know I must see what the dark place wants to show me."

"Even though you don't want to?"

Claudia sighed. "Even though I don't want to."

———

Pilate held up his goblet for more wine, and a servant promptly appeared and filled his cup. Claudia reclined across from her husband and nibbled on a fresh fig.

"Husband, what's troubling you?"

Pilate drank deeply and looked at his wife. "It's more a matter of what's not. These Jews are a raucous bunch. Stubborn and cantankerous. Always plotting and scheming."

Claudia took a sip of wine. "Sounds a lot like Rome."

Pilate grimaced the hint of a smile. "Don't try to cheer me up. It won't work this time. The infernal heat, dust, sour wine…this place is the scourge of civilization. What I wouldn't give for a Roman bath."

"A Roman bath…." Claudia replied. "What wonderful times Livia, Cornelia, Julia, and I had at the baths! Still, the quarters Herod has arranged for us here in his palace are quite respectable."

Pilate looked at his wife with an arched eyebrow. "I don't know about that. Herod's palace is second-rate compared to Rome. I'd take a Roman villa anytime. And then you throw in the Pharisees and Caiaphas, the schemer of all schemers. He and the rest of them wear their religion on their sleeve. It's not like they have our Roman gods at their disposal. They just have the one, and one is all Caiaphas needs to keep everyone riled up especially during Passover."

"I thought you liked Caiaphas," Claudia replied, reaching for a stuffed date.

"Tolerate is more like it. I can work with Caiaphas, most of the time. That's not to say I like him or, for that matter, trust or even respect him. He never lets up, constantly pushing for more. Usually in the name of religion, but always for himself or his friends. And now he's conjured up another so-called threat to, as he calls it, 'the Roman rule of law.'" Pilate laughed sarcastically as he clapped his hands for more wine. "The only threat he's concerned about is anything, real or imagined, that might challenge his and the Pharisees' power. In fact, I've got to meet with him again tomorrow about the latest and greatest threat."

Claudia wiped her hands on a napkin. "Another zealot?"

"Maybe, maybe not. Sometimes it's hard to tell the difference with these people," Pilate replied, brushing the crumbs from dinner off his tunic. "Maybe it's Barabbas. He claims to be a zealot, but even the Jews don't like him. Appears he has quite a temper and is quick to use his sword on whoever crosses him." Pilate reached for a piece of salted fish. "Oh, yes, I almost forgot. Rumor has it that there's one other fellow that Caiaphas has it in for. Some wandering, country boy from Nazareth."

Claudia took a sip of water. "Is he violent like Barabbas?"

"Don't know for sure," replied Pilate between mouthfuls of fish. "Seems like I heard from Telemarchus that he was some sort of self-styled rabbi who goes around with a small band of followers talking to poor country folk like himself. Whoever it is, I'll find out from Caiaphas tomorrow. I can hardly wait."

Pilate tossed the remains of the fish he was eating on the platter in front of him in disgust. "They can't even prepare common food like a simple piece of salted fish. What I'd give for some Roman food—fresh grapes, pork sausages, cheese and some decent bread, not to mention a liter of real wine."

Claudia reached over and stroked her husband's hand. "Remember when we were invited to the dinner party at Maximus and Cornelia's?"

Pilate nodded as he searched for an olive.

"What an evening," Claudia continued. "A warm summer breeze. The roasted peacock was a real delicacy and the apricots, peaches, and cherries."

In spite of himself, Pilate got caught up in Claudia's wistful memory. "The oysters were the best I ever tasted." His scowl quickly returned. "A pleasant but distant memory—a civilized time and place Jerusalem and its inhabitants have no acquaintance with."

The following morning found Claudia and Miriam strolling through one of Herod's gardens. Miriam touched one of the blossoming plants. "The garden smells fragrant and fresh."

Claudia bent over and smelled one of the blossoms, then walked over to a stone bench and sat down. She folded her hands in her lap and stared at the distant hills.

Miriam sat down beside her. "What troubles you, Mistress?"

"I had another dream last night."

"Was it like the others?"

Claudia looked at the stone tiles beneath her feet. "It was similar, but different. The dreams are becoming more frequent. In each dream, I am older and drawing closer to the dark place." Claudia wiped a bead of sweat from her forehead. "I will soon arrive at a place I don't want to go."

As his servant adjusted his breastplate, Pilate accepted the goblet of wine Claudia offered him. "Well, today's the big day, my dear. As soon as I clear things up with Caiaphas and the riff-raff from the Sanhedrin, you and I will be on our way to Caesarea. Wish me luck."

Draining the last of the wine from his goblet, Pilate turned to his adjutant. "Telemarchus, who's the unlucky dolt on Caiaphas' hit list this time?"

Telemarchus took one last look at the scroll listing the business at hand. "I hear it will either be the murderer Barabbas or the fellow from Nazareth. I forget his name."

Claudia turned to Miriam and whispered, "My husband is often ill-tempered when he returns from meeting with the Sanhedrin. Find the best wine, bread, and cheese you can. He will have little appetite but a large thirst."

Miriam nodded and quickly left to do her mistress' bidding.

It was late afternoon when Pilate returned from meeting in the Sanhedrin in a flurry, Telemarchus following close behind.

"Wine, and plenty of it!" Pilate shouted at the hapless servants, sending his helmet clattering across the tiled floor. He drank deeply from the goblet his nervous attendant had just poured, while another servant removed his breastplate and still another offered him a basin of fresh water and a clean towel. Pilate handed his empty goblet to the wine attendant to refill while he washed and dried his hands and face.

Flinging the towel at the hapless servant, he snatched the fresh goblet of wine from the attendant's hand and plopped down in a heavy chair made of cedar.

"Have you ever seen anything to beat it, Telemarchus?"

"It's as you have said many times, Governor. The Jews are very zealous regarding their religion and politics," Telemarchus replied as he accepted a goblet of wine from one of the servants.

Pilate called for a wet towel. "Accusing that fellow, Jesus of Nazareth, of being a malefactor. How ridiculous is that?" Wiping the perspiration from his face with the cool, damp towel, Pilate continued. "You were there when I took him into the palace and examined him. Do you think he's guilty of sedition and preventing the payment of tribute, not to mention a threat to Tiberius or, for that matter, even Caiaphas?"

Telemarchus stroked his chin. "One of my agents did hear him once say, 'Render unto Caesar what is Caesar's and to God what is God's.'"

Pilate dropped the towel to the floor. "Doesn't sound like a threat to me. And he also said his kingdom is not of this world, which is the only world that I or the Emperor is concerned with. He can be king of all the imaginary worlds he wants as long as he makes no claims on the real one."

Telemarchus smiled. "It is hard to see Jesus of Nazareth as a threat to the world of the Empire."

Pilate massaged his temples. "I'll tell you another thing, Telemarchus. He didn't have the mannerisms of a guilty man. The guilty will sing like a canary, tell you whatever they think you want to hear. This Jesus of Nazareth was calm and collected. I found it a little unsettling."

"You did a wise thing, Governor, by sending Jesus to Herod Antipas on jurisdictional grounds. It buys time and shifts the burden of responsibility to Herod."

Pilate nodded. "The bottom line is that I could find no fault with this Jesus. Bring me Barabbas and I'll take care of him in quick order."

Telemarchus raised his goblet in agreement and drank the last of his wine.

———

The moon was but a sliver, offering just enough light to see the path. There was no breeze but rather a cool stillness. As Claudia climbed the hill to the dark place, her breathing became more labored. She wanted to run but felt the pull of what lay ahead.

Rising before her out of the darkness was a single, wooden cross. As she approached, Claudia could hear the moans of suffering from the person nailed to it. Standing before the cross, Claudia kept her head down, staring at the bloodied feet. She didn't want to look up but found her eyes following the line of torment from the feet to the knees to the pierced side and finally to a face she knew would be contorted in agony.

Claudia was surprised at what she saw. Although the face looking down at her bore the marks of torture, the moaning stopped. The eyes were clear and calm with compassion. She felt bathed in the look of those eyes.

Claudia awoke with a startled cry.

———

It was late in the evening. The air was pungent with the smell of the olive oil lamps and the charcoal stove on the terrace. Claudia stared at her husband.

"I got your message this morning before the proceedings started, about the dreams and your warning not to bring harm to Jesus of Nazareth."

Claudia shifted her gaze to the glowing charcoal embers. "He was innocent and he had great power."

Pilate leaned over and stirred the fire with a poker, sending embers blinking up into the night sky. "I know he was innocent, my dear. But he was only a man who met an unfortunate end due to pragmatic political realities."

Claudia looked at Pilate. "I'm not so sure."

"Not so sure of what?" Pilate replied.

"He knew me. He was suffering, but he was more than his suffering."

Pilate gave his wife a consoling smile. "Well, he was on a cross, and crucifixion is a painful death."

Claudia's eyes glistened. "I know the cross he was on is a place of pain and death, but in a strange way I felt he had the power to leave the cross if he wanted to. He wasn't just dying on the cross—he was also living on the cross."

Pilate stood up and stretched. "Enough with the dreams. It's been a long day. I did what I could to spare Jesus of Nazareth. One of the last things he said to me was that he came to testify to the truth. That everyone on the side of truth would listen to him. Well, I can vouch for one thing: the crowd he was testifying to certainly was not listening—to him or me. Anyway, it's like I said to him, 'What is truth?' The truth is his own people wanted him dead. Couldn't believe they chose to free that murderer, Barabbas, but then…we are in Jerusalem. Besides, you know as well as I do that I don't need to risk my position by having Caiaphas and his bunch running to Vitellius and complaining again. That's why I had the basin of water brought to the judgment seat and washed my hands of the whole sorry mess."

"Some things are more easily washed away than others," Claudia replied as she rose from her chair.

Pilate was taken aback by Claudia's assertiveness, and none too pleased with it. "I'll finish the rest of my business here within the week. Then we will leave for Caesarea. Everything will look better once we have shaken off the dust of Jerusalem."

Claudia lay on her couch, unable to sleep even after Miriam had brought her a small bowl of warm milk.

"Is there anything else I can do for you, Mistress? Perhaps some ointment or incense to ease your spirit?"

Claudia motioned for Miriam to come sit on the side of her couch. "It's the dreams, Miriam. I am haunted by the man in my dreams. He is the one, Jesus, who was crucified today. He is a man I don't even know, but who knows me. A man unlike any other. Does it sound to you like I'm losing my senses?"

Miriam pulled the coverlet around Claudia's legs. "No, Mistress. I don't think you are losing your senses."

The two women sat in silence, listening to the night sounds of the streets below.

"Mistress?"

"Yes, Miriam."

"Would you like to know more about the man called Jesus?"

Claudia grasped Miriam by the hand. "Is that possible?"

"Perhaps. I know some of his followers. Would you like for me to make an inquiry?

"Yes, Miriam, I would."

Miriam rose from the couch. "I will do as you wish in the morning. Good night, Mistress."

Claudia lay back on her couch. She wondered what his followers might reveal about the man called Jesus. It would be risky to meet with them, but the dream still haunted her. And there was the rumor that he would rise again.

As she drifted off to sleep, Claudia felt a gentle breeze of possibility sweep over her.

COMMENTS

Matthew 27

Claudia had troubling dreams and warned her husband, a warning he didn't heed. While Pilate would have preferred to put Barabbas to death, he didn't lose any sleep over sacrificing Jesus in order to satisfy Caiaphas and his mob. Sometimes, the ends had to justify the means. As far as Pilate was concerned, the best he could say about the Israelites was that they were a contentious and rabble-rousing lot.

Claudia felt differently. She had a sensitive side. Still, she wasn't a Jew but a Roman. She tried to intervene, but was it enough? It did not stop her husband from having Jesus crucified, but was it enough to point her toward a different path?

Pragmatism and intuition are two themes that can be found in this story —the pragmatic expediency of Pilate in contrast with the intuitive instincts of his wife, Claudia. History suggests that Pilate was not a particularly thoughtful governor, but instead, had an abrasive and even abusive reputation—one that found crucifixion an easy enough sanction to render. We know even less about his wife, Claudia, except for that brief yet powerful and enigmatic passage imploring her husband to bring no harm to "that just man," Jesus.

There are examples throughout history and in everyday life where a wife's softer, sensitive side takes the edge off the aggressiveness of a husband's hard line of decision-making, be it in business or in family matters. It seems that Pilate would have preferred Barabbas on the cross rather than Jesus, since he did make more of an effort to spare him than he typically would have, perhaps due to his wife's influence. It also seems clear that while puzzled, perhaps even somewhat exasperated, Pilate was impressed with the calm demeanor of Jesus. Still, he was a Roman bureaucrat trying to maintain order and provide governance in a place he didn't understand or want to be. Pilate was well-acquainted with Roman law and, even more so, political compromise.

Pilate might as well have "held his nose" as he symbolically "washed his hands" before acceding to the demands of the Jewish leaders. He did what savvy political bureaucrats often do even today: cover himself, pass the buck, and so forth. He didn't want another uprising or the Jewish leaders sending envoys to complain about him to his superiors. His wife is another matter. We really don't know that much about her. Had she heard about Jesus of Nazareth from one of her servants or other acquaintances? Had her dreams been troubling her for some time or was her attempted intervention on behalf of Jesus the result of a single, troubling episode? In the end, Claudia tried to intervene while Pilate chose the expedient path of least resistance. He knew better but did nothing.

We all have a little Pilate in us and not enough Claudia. We are quick enough to do the right thing when everyone is on board. When we are in the minority, we either remain quiet for fear of being criticized or join the lynch mob even though we know better. As followers of Christ, we need to get used to being in the minority as we seek to act in truth and love. The expedient path often leads to disappointment and suffering, while the long way can often teach us patience, humility, and perseverance.

QUESTIONS

1. Using your imagination, if Pilate had released Jesus and crucified Barabbas, what do you think the consequences would have been for him? For Jesus?

2. Pilate followed the rule of law and legal tradition yet didn't do the right thing. Is that also true on occasion in today's world? Can we confuse what is legal with what is moral? Can the law be adhered to and still allow a terrible injustice to occur? Can you think of any examples from the "civil rights" era, or more recently, where persons on death row were found to be innocent?

3. Can you think of any times where you or someone you know was harmed by bureaucratic insensitivity or unfairness in the workplace or other setting?

4. Have we ever used the law or an organization or agency's bureaucratic process to compromise or sacrifice the welfare of someone else for the sake of expediency in improving our own position?

NOTES:

_____

_____

_____

_____

_____

_____

_____

_____

Interview with Joab

_____

_____

_____

_____

_____

_____

13

REMEMBER ME

I T'S HOT AS blazes," the Roman soldier said to Marcus, the centurion in charge of the day's executions.

Marcus turned and looked at the sky. *Dark clouds coming in from the west. Might bring a storm…but not likely.*

The soldier's gaze followed the centurion's. "Not many storms this time of year. We should be through before dark. Just three this time, and the crowd's not that large. Not like last time when we had to do a dozen."

Marcus nodded in agreement. "Pilate's definitely partial to Golgotha. Even though he rarely comes to Jerusalem, he had more than two hundred crucified by this time last year."

"Wasn't that when the village down in the Jordan valley rebelled against the extra tax on grain?"

Marcus took off his helmet and wiped the sweat from his brow. "That's the one. Like I said, our procurator has always favored the cross when it comes to punishment."

Putting on his helmet, the centurion walked down from the rise where he had been observing the crowd to check on the condition of the three condemned men. He had witnessed crucifixions more times than he could remember during his years of service to the Emperor. It went with the territory. Killing, whether on the battlefield or the cross, was part of his job. Still, in Marcus' mind, this one seemed different. The man in the middle— the one they called Jesus—didn't claim to be innocent or guilty. He just stood there in silence when Pilate passed judgment on him. Even Pilate, who seemed to have a taste for sending people to the cross, acted like he was looking for a way to spare this Jesus fellow. But old Caiaphas and his boys made sure the crowd kept up the pressure, so that in the end, the procurator folded.

As Marcus walked among the crowd, he took in a sight that he had seen countless times before—women wringing their hands and crying. And of course, there were several whoops and cat-calls from the Sanhedrin, taunting the man called Jesus, shouting at him to save himself if he was truly the Christ, God's chosen one. Marcus smiled to himself. *These were the kind of men who like to finish off the wounded in battle. You never seem to be able to locate them in the presence of a well-armed, evenly matched opponent. But at the end of the battle, they seem to come out of the woodwork to finish off the helpless and the dying.*

To his left, three of his guards were casting lots for the garments of the Nazarene. Cratus, the youngest, approached Marcus. "Look, I won it. And a purple robe, at that. Not bad for the likes of him."

Marcus simply looked at Cratus. It didn't take much to excite the young.

The other two soldiers began to join in with the Sanhedrin crowd, mocking the Nazarene. "King of the Jews, come down from your cross and save yourself!"

Even one of the two thieves—the one on the right, joined in. "If you are the Christ, save yourself and us!"

Marcus rubbed the stubble on his chin. *Not bad. Go for the long shot. Just in case. Half a jeer and half a desperate hope and plea. Jesus of Nazareth, save yourself, and save me as well.* The centurion could feel the beginning of a headache.

After checking the condition of the three crucified men, Marcus shouted, "Cratus, get over here and dip a sponge into that jar of wine and raise it to the lips of the Nazarene."

Cratus stuck a sponge on the end of his spear. "What about the other two?"

"Leave them be for now. This one is about done. He's asked for some water, so wet his lips with the wine. His day will soon be over. And Cratus?"

"Yes, Centurion?"

"When you get through with that, take some water over to those women. I think one of them must be his mother."

Cratus grinned. "You're getting soft, sir. Never seen you worry about thirsty mourners, family or no family."

One look from Marcus was all it took to wipe the smile from Cratus' face and send him scurrying to carry out his orders.

An elderly man called out to Marcus, "Centurion, what do you think of the man Jesus? Is he a king, a fool, or a criminal like the other two?"

Marcus looked at the old man and replied, "How would I know? I'm not the judge, only the executioner."

"You didn't join in with the other soldiers and Pharisees," the old man continued. "I was curious about that."

The centurion gave the old man a stern look. "Curiosity can get you in trouble."

The old man offered the hint of a smile. "Indeed, it has and will more than likely be the case in the future."

Marcus cleared his threat. His head was beginning to throb. "The man called Jesus may not be a king, but neither is he a criminal. I've crucified a lot of men, but never anyone like him. He bears his suffering like an innocent man, like he is doing it for someone else, although I have no idea who that might be. He dies like others die on the cross, but he doesn't complain."

Suddenly the thief on the right stepped up his ridicule of the Nazarene, perhaps as a way to take his mind off his own pain. The thief to the left had said little in the last hour, so Marcus took notice when he interrupted his partner in crime in mid-sentence.

"Shut up, Hiram! Shut up for God's sake! You and I are guilty of the crimes that have led us to this place. This man has done nothing wrong. Didn't you just hear him ask his father to forgive even those who are killing him?"

The speaker raised his head with great effort to look at Jesus. "If you can get God to forgive the ones who are killing you, maybe you can ask him to forgive me. Maybe you can even remember me—remember me when you come into your kingdom."

Marcus listened intently.

With labored breathing, Jesus turned to the thief. "Today, you will be with me in paradise."

The old man sidled up to Marcus. "Will you remember, Centurion? Will you remember this man and this day?"

Marcus pondered the question before responding. "I will. I will remember this day."

Then he turned and walked away.

COMMENTS

Luke 23:26-42

When someone dies, even of natural causes, sorrow and remembering follow. Executions create a rawer experience where grief hangs heavy and emotions may be mixed. Mary, the mother of Jesus, and His followers wept and mourned His loss. Perhaps His accusers felt a measure of relief and satisfaction. The thieves shared a common fate with Jesus—at least for the moment. Their reactions demonstrate how persons experiencing common suffering can have very different outcomes, depending on how they choose to respond to their situation.

And there was the centurion, the one responsible for carrying out Pilate's orders. Although death was an experience he was well acquainted with, this time it was different in that the death of Jesus was in some way extraordinary.

How would we react if we were in the crowd? Would we remain silent for fear of being identified as one of Jesus' followers or would we even be there at all? Would we be hiding out like most of the other disciples?

An even more cogent point has to do with the two thieves. Would we be more like the first one, calling for Jesus to save himself *and* us, or more like the second thief, admitting our guilt and confessing His innocence, asking only to be remembered? How do we respond to times of profound loss and grief? What do we remember?

In the end, how we respond to death may depend on our relationship to the one who has died.

QUESTIONS

1. How do you think you would have felt if you were the centurion in charge? What kind of impact do you feel the death of Jesus would have had on you?

2. Which of the two thieves do you feel you would have been most like in terms of their reactions? Can you identify with both of them? Are we more likely to complain and demand deliverance from our hardship and suffering, or do we become more humble and ask to be remembered?

3. Can you remember the death of loved ones in your life? Did you feel at peace with the relationship, or was there unfinished business between you and the one who died? If there were unresolved conflicts, how can you make peace with them now?

NOTES:

_____

_____

_____

_____

_____

_____

_____

_____

_____

_____

14

TRUE BELIEVER

THE AFTERNOON WAS hot and dusty. A group of concerned priests and community leaders gathered in the courtyard of the synagogue and talked among themselves. These pious men were well aware of the constant threat and corrupting influence of self-proclaimed false messiahs and competing religious movements. Israel had failed on more than one occasion to remain true to God's direction and had paid a heavy price of sorrow and suffering. From Jeremiah to Amos, prophets had warned and wept their way through Israel's history. The men knew it was up to them to remain ever-vigilant if Israel was to stay on the straight and narrow path.

Hezeriah placed both hands on the shoulders of the young man standing in front of him. "Saul, you represent the future of our faith. If we can recruit more men with the fervor and commitment you have, Israel's future will be bright indeed."

The men surrounding Hezeriah and Saul enthusiastically voiced their approval.

Ebenezer slapped Saul on the back. "Young man, you have made us proud. From Ashdod to Ashkelon and other places as well, you have been a one man army for God, rooting out those blasphemous Christians. They are filling up our prisons thanks to you. They will either repent and return to the true faith or face the consequences."

Saul offered Ebenezer a serious smile. "I appreciate your confidence and support, but you must know that it takes teamwork to cut out the cancer before it spreads. As much as your prayers and moral support mean to our efforts, it is your financial support that allows me and my associates to pay informers. Many of the Christians meet in secret. Without the means to reward their neighbors and fellow workers for vital information, our rate of apprehension and arrest would be much lower."

"You have our full financial backing—whatever you need," Hezeriah asserted. "We have even included a designated 'defending the faith' tithing category as part of our outreach and political action ministry. Don't worry about the money, my young friend—just keep up the good work."

"That's right," Ebenezer chimed in, "without the intelligence you provide through your contacts, we could not have eliminated one of the biggest threats that we have faced." The others voiced their approval as Ebenezer continued. "That Stephen was a slick one, coming to our community under the guise of helping the poor and then insulting the Church Council in this very synagogue. Calling us stiffnecked, persecutors of the prophets—even murderers."

The men shouted their indignities as Hezeriah clapped his hands for the servants. Wine was poured and offered to the gathering.

"Time for a little refreshment," Hezeriah said, "and a celebration of defeating the enemy."

As the men drank, Hezeriah commented, "Stephen is the first of the Christian apostles to be stoned."

"But he won't be the last," Saul replied. "He brought it on himself."

One of the men, John, who had said nothing during the meeting, spoke up. "I have to say, Stephen took the stoning like a man."

Simon Jonas added, "I'll also confess that I was troubled when Stephen's last words were to ask God to not charge his death against us—to forgive us for what we were doing to him."

Murmurs ran through the group, giving some measure of credence to Simon Jonas' concerns.

Saul spoke clearly and forcefully. "The man, Stephen, may have been misguided—brainwashed if you willrather than harboring evil intent. He may have even been a good man by some measure. In the end, it doesn't matter. Either way, the outcome is equally dangerous—the erosion of our religious values and national identity. The same could be said about Jesus of Nazareth whom he followed. However and wherever such threats come from, they must be eliminated. If the Stephens of this world can't love and support our traditions, then they need to leave our midst and our land—or face the consequences."

"Here, here!" shouted Ebenezer. "A toast to Saul for his virtue and steadfastness."

Cups were raised and food was eaten throughout the afternoon on into the evening. As the evening grew late, Saul got the group's attention.

"Friends and supporters, I must now retire. I need my rest for the journey to Damascus tomorrow."

After Saul said his goodbyes to his supporters, Hezeriah walked him to the street. Embracing Saul, Hezeriah smiled. "I couldn't be prouder of you if you were my own son. God be with you."

"And with you, Hezeriah," Saul replied. "I will see you and the others within the week. I am confident my work in Damascus won't take long."

COMMENTS

Acts: 6:8, 8:1-3

Saul was a bright, energetic man who passionately defended the religious establishment of his day. He was of the tribe of Benjamin and a Pharisee, and a Roman citizen as well. He worked diligently to root out heretical movements, including one of the most recent threats, the followers of Christ.

The apostle Stephen was drawn to what Jesus taught and how He ministered to the poor. During one of Stephen's early efforts to help the poor and spread the good news of Christ, he ran afoul of local religious leaders. Baited by a crowd which may well have included Saul's band of agitators in a hearing before their council, he defended his actions and offended their sensibilities. Stephen enraged the crowd by offering them a bluntly accurate description of how they had treated God's prophets throughout their history. Furious, the mob dragged Stephen to a place where they stoned him to death. Saul participated in the death of Stephen, as well as the torture and imprisonment of other Christians who refused to recant their faith.

In the eyes of the local religious establishment, Saul was a rising star who acted in defense of their traditions. He was a true believer who did his duty, and did it with great effectiveness.

When Saul began his journey to Damascus, he had no idea where that journey was going to take him. God got his attention and he responded. As a "true believer" in the religious traditions of his day, Paul had defended those traditions to the point of imprisoning and even participating in the murder of innocent persons who thought and believed differently from him. That was the "bad news." The "good news" is that Saul's story doesn't end there any more than our story ends when we use our religious beliefs to encourage prejudice, fear, and even hatred. We may not literally imprison people who don't believe like we do or participate in their murder. Yet, through malicious gossip and prejudice, we can "kill" their reputation and good name, and we can isolate them from the fellowship they need in order to feel loved and cared for.

The proud incarcerator and killer of Christians named Saul became the humble and determined messenger for Christ named Paul, spreading the good news of liberation and transformation. How did that happen? It happened with Paul just as it happens with us—something happens in us and to us in one way or another that transforms us from being a "true believer" in this or that political, religious, or philosophical tradition to a "believer in the truth" of Christ.

Like Paul, when it happens, we are never the same again.

QUESTIONS

1. Can you look back and remember when you were younger and so certain and sure of everything? How have your experiences through the years changed your attitude? Changed you?

2. When God gets our attention and calls us to do something, do we have to act? What are our choices? What are the consequences for our choices?

3. Have you ever experienced people in your fellowship or church who were fervent believers in their faith and treated anyone who differed with them dismissively or even cruelly? How does such behavior impact a church or group of spiritual seekers?

4. Although the two ideas are not mutually exclusive, what do you feel is the difference between "true believers" and "believers in the truth"? Which group is more likely to defend and which one is more likely to seek?

NOTES:

_____

_____

_____

_____

_____

_____

_____

_____

_____

_____

_____

_____

_____

_____

_____

15

DEFENDER OF THE FAITH

T HE EVENING AIR was more humid than normal as the members of the Sanhedrin filed out of the meeting hall. They left as they came, some alone, others talking in small groups. Nicodemus gathered up his cloak and looked at the hallowed halls for what he suspected was his last time. It had been a typical meeting, the tedious details of governance mixed with a pompous speech or two, along with a dash of anti-Pilate and Caesar rhetoric. It always boiled down to the same thing—how to stay in power, help one's friends, and punish one's enemies.

Of course, the Sanhedrin also included a few good men, men like Lucas and Phillip who were more interested in finding provisions for the poor than increasing their own status. Such men, unfortunately, were the exception rather than the rule.

As Nicodemus made his way toward the entrance, he heard someone calling his name. Turning, he saw Caiaphas hurrying toward him.

"Nicodemus. May I have a word with you before you leave?"

Nicodemus nodded as Caiaphas beckoned him to sit and talk.

"Dear Nicodemus, I have heard a disturbing rumor that you are planning to resign your seat on the Sanhedrin."

"You have heard correctly, Caiaphas. I have served long enough—perhaps too long."

"That is not true, my friend. You have never been needed more than now. You are a breath of fresh air in a room full of hot air, not the least of which I provide," Caiaphas replied with a smile.

Nicodemus said nothing.

"You have a reputation for integrity and kindness," Caiaphas continued. "Your sweet spirit has reconciled so many disputes among our members. Everyone respects you, including me. No one provides a balance point between the different interests during these difficult and challenging times more than you."

"You are good with words, Caiaphas. You always have been. I am more awkward than you in speech. My heart is what leads me. My heart is no match for your mind's agility, and my heart is tired."

Caiaphas's gaze softened as he looked at Nicodemus. "We have known each other since we were boys studying under old Rabbi Meshach. You were always the sensitive scholar, and I was the political pragmatist. You felt—I thought. Where you were careful, I was bold. You, my friend, have always been a dreamer. For better or worse, I'm a realist. We are different sides of Israel's coin. Both sides are needed. Your heart is needed as much as my action. Nicodemus, don't you realize that you are the heart of the Sanhedrin?"

Nicodemus smiled sadly. "My old friend Caiaphas. Your words are sweeter than honey. I have always marveled at the way you have with words. But as nice as your compliments might be, their sheen dulls against the contradictions of an old man's life. I fear my old heart is more than tired. I believe it is also broken."

"You are just tired, Nicodemus. A season's rest and you will be good as new. We need you—Israel needs you. We have never been at a more critical time in Israel's history than now," Caiaphas replied in earnest. "You know that you and I and the rest of the Sanhedrin are the only thing standing between Roman brutality and our people."

Nicodemus shook his head. "A broken body can mend in time. A broken heart is different. In time, it loses hope. I fear that we are becoming more like the Romans—that we are losing our memory of the past, of the promises we made and haven't kept."

Caiaphas was becoming more exasperated.

"Are you still mourning the death of that country preacher, Jesus? You know as well as I how many false messiahs we have had to deal with. Every con-artist magician and wild-eyed zealot has tried to cash in on that title. Can't you remember all the close calls, all the times hardedged Roman governors like Pilate were about to shed our people's blood? If we hadn't cooperated—if we didn't hand over the troublemakers to them—who knows how many lives would have been lost? None of us may have survived. I don't like handing any Jew over to the Romans no matter how crazy or criminal they are. But sacrifices have to be made. I don't have to tell you how difficult it is maintain control under the likes of Pilate. I have to deal with him all the time. Nothing comes easy from him. Pilate begrudges us and our people any advantage we seek. He has little administrative or diplomatic ability and even less interest. If it wasn't for his adjutant, Telemarchus, nothing would ever get done. And if one dares cross the line with him—no matter how just or noble the cause, Pilate doesn't hesitate to react punitively, and often with violence. He actually likes crucifixion and has proved that point more than any other governor I can remember in my lifetime. I personally don't like crucifixion except for the most violent of offenders. But it is a reality and, sometimes, the lesser of evils."

Nicodemus' steady gaze unnerved Caiaphas. "You chose Jesus over Barabbas, a known murderer. How can that be? How can you send a man who heals the sick, comforts the afflicted, and preaches peace to the cross and set one who robs the poor, murders the wayfarer, and advocates violence free? How is that possible?"

Caiaphas shrugged. "I know it's hard—that it makes no sense in the recesses of the heart. But as soft as the heart needs to be, in difficult times, the mind must sometimes steel itself to the reality at hand—to 'what is' rather than 'what might be.'"

"Caiaphas, Caiaphas. What are you saying?" Nicodemus replied, throwing his hands up in dismay. "Jesus never threatened Rome or you. He clearly stated his kingdom was not of this world. His message was one of hope and compassion, not violence. He advocated a change of the heart, not a change of regime."

Caiaphas sighed and smiled wearily. "Poor Nicodemus. Can't you see? The change Jesus stood for is the most dangerous change of all. Give me a Barabbas to deal with any day. The Barabbases of this world are clear in their desires. Force meets force and they disappear. A Jesus of love and peace and forgiveness—who knows where that would end and what it might lead to?"

Nicodemus rose to leave. "Caiaphas, my prayers will be with you and the other members of the Sanhedrin."

Rising to his feet as well, Caiaphas called one last time to Nicodemus as he walked toward the doorway. "Remember the passion you had at the beginning? How you and I and others wanted to make a difference in the lives of our people? It hasn't been perfect, but we have succeeded in many ways. Remember that, Nicodemus. Remember."

Nicodemus stopped at the doorway and turned toward Caiaphas.

"I do remember, Caiaphas. I remember wanting to make a difference. But this is not the difference I wanted to make."

COMMENTS

John 3:1-21; John 7:50-52; John 18:12-14; John 19:6-7.15-16, 28-40

Sometimes hard decisions have to be made. Sometimes individuals like Jesus have to be sacrificed for the greater good—especially when those individuals threaten longheld, sacred traditions.

Caiaphas had a lot on his mind: an iron-fisted Roman governor, self-proclaimed messiahs popping up everywhere, and zealots fomenting open rebellion with the Roman garrison that was sure to end in defeat and even more hardship. Caiaphas was not only a religious leader; he was also an administrator who had to keep his pulse on the politics of the day. Perhaps his most important task was to manage expectations—his people's, the Romans', and especially the Sanhedrin's.

In the story, rumor had it that Nicodemus was about to resign, and Caiaphas could not afford to let that happen. He needed Nicodemus. It was clear Nicodemus had a soft spot for Jesus of Nazareth. That was unfortunate, but with Jesus' execution, it was in the past. At least, Caiaphas hoped so.

It is easy enough to forget that it was the religious establishment of his day that chose Jesus for the cross rather than Barabbas. Caiaphas and his pious friends had been gunning for Jesus, nipping at His heels every chance they got, trying to trick Him or trap Him one way or another with some kind of theological mistake or religious impropriety. From Jesus' dining with riff-raff like Matthew the tax collector to defending a woman caught in the act of adultery, the undaunted enthusiasm of the Pharisees was only surpassed by their ineptitude. Like well-educated keystone cops, they understood the letter of the Law, but not the spirit.

Of course, they finally got what they wanted: Jesus nailed to a cross. But they couldn't keep Him there. Truth doesn't go quietly into the night.

Caiaphas was their leader. He quarterbacked their strategy and managed all the minutiae, from the thirty pieces of silver to the relentless chorus of "Crucify Him!" Yet, in his mind he did it for the greater good of the religious order. Sometimes one has to dirty one's hands to keep religion pure.

Of course, Nicodemus was not buying into that kind of logic. As a member of the Sanhedrin, he tried to, but it just didn't stick. Nicodemus wanted to be born into something new—new hope and a new voice.

Caiaphas would have none of Nicodemus's vision. He couldn't afford to. Too much was at stake, including his own position and worldview. For Caiaphas, the world remained flat. The old ways were safest. The straight and narrow of past tradition was the way to go.

Like many of us today, Caiaphas was stuck in the legalism of tradition. Can we honor our traditions and be open to something more? That is what Nicodemus yearned for. The heart, as does the Holy Spirit, blows where it will. Can we both honor tradition and follow the Holy Spirit to new and places unknown? That is the challenge that Caiaphas failed and Nicodemus embraced.

What will we do?

QUESTIONS

1. We see Caiaphas as a villain and rightly so. Yet we can speculate on what motivated him. What led him to see Jesus as the enemy? Why do you think he felt so threatened by Jesus' ministry?

2. Why was Nicodemus different from Caiaphas? What traits and characteristics did Nicodemus possess that Caiaphas didn't?

3. How might you and I be a little like Caiaphas? Do we have problems with people different from us, with a change in the order of worship or a ministry different from what we are accustomed to?

4. How can we be more like Nicodemus, more open to the unexpected "voice of God"?

NOTES:

_____

_____

_____

_____

_____

_____

_____

_____

_____

_____

ABOUT THE AUTHOR

A FORMER PRISON PSYCHOLOGIST, Michael Braswell has earned four degrees in psychology and counseling from Mercer University, the University of Georgia and a PhD from the University of Southern Mississippi. He has taught criminal justice ethics and human relations for more than thirty years. He is currently Professor Emeritus at East Tennessee State University.

Michael has published 20 books, including "Morality Stories" (with Joy Pollock and Scott Braswell) and "Justice, Crime and Ethics" (with Bernard and Belinda McCarthy). His writing has focused on peacemaking and justice issues as well as the spiritual journey.

Married for more than 40 years, he and his wife, Susan, work together as publishing consultants and are active in their Baptist church.

www.ingramcontent.com/pod-product-compliance
Lightning Source LLC
Chambersburg PA
CBHW070040030726
47506CB00003B/814